Diamond cursed inwardly, his gut aching from the woman's knee jab. Where was she in this murky water? He dove deeper until he caught a glimpse of her. It wasn't *his* fault she kept fighting him! Didn't she realize he'd dived in to rescue her when she went overboard?

He wrapped himself around her like a vise, and withstood her struggles. They broke the surface at the same time. "Let go of those suitcases!" he gasped.

"They're worth a fortune," Tamara said, determined to hold on to the passenger's luggage.

He tugged the hair away from her face, to get a look at her. She was *gorgeous!*

"Ow," she complained. "Quit trying to drown me!"

Tightening his grip, he slammed a hard kiss against her lips, trying to tell himself he just wanted to shut her up.

Dear Reader,

We love to travel. We even enjoy packing, making arrangements for the children, our husbands, our pets—everything that adds to the sense of impending adventure. And adventure is exactly what we found sailing the Carribean and the route taken by the *Diamond Queen* in Tamara and Michael's story.

Cruisin' Mr. Diamond is the third of our cruise trilogy, Ports of Call. Here's hoping all your travels are as happy as ours have been!

Love,

Lynn Leslie

Lynn Leslie

CRUISIN'
MR. DIAMOND

Harlequin Books

TORONTO • NEW YORK • LONDON
AMSTERDAM • PARIS • SYDNEY • HAMBURG
STOCKHOLM • ATHENS • TOKYO • MILAN
MADRID • WARSAW • BUDAPEST • AUCKLAND

Thanks, "Days" and "G.H.," for the peeks
behind the scenes. Thanks in particular to
John Riley—your help was especially appreciated.

ISBN 0-373-16551-X

CRUISIN' MR. DIAMOND

Copyright © 1994 by Sherrill Bodine and Elaine Sima.

Day One—Embarkation—Miami

"Diamond! Diamond! We want Diamond on the *Diamond!*"

The chant from the crowd on the dock swelled to alarming proportions as it rolled up the *Diamond Queen*'s gangplank to Tamara Hayes's ears.

"I'll give him to you on a silver platter if he ever gets here," she muttered under her breath.

A louder roar, as if collectively the fans had taken a deep breath to vocalize at full lung capacity, stopped her in midstride. What had the S&B Steamship Line gotten her into this time?

Deafened by the cacophony of eager voices, she had to lean against John Pardue's pristine white jacket to hear what he was saying. "What?" she shouted over the din.

"I said, Captain Swevsen commands that you handle this."

Tilting her head, she glared up at him. "But you're the purser. It's your job to deal with passenger requests."

He widened his eyes in mock horror and took one unsteady step back. "No way! You're the activities director. This soap opera cruise group is your baby! Ciao!"

He bolted before she could grab hold of his arm and she found herself shouting into thin air. "I'll get you for this!" She had enthusiastically agreed with the concept of having daytime television stars aboard when it was presented, but she'd had no idea of the reception that Michael Shannon would generate. After all, the man was only a soap opera star—not the President!

She groaned in frustration as she watched John disappear into the cocktail lounge, where it was blissfully cool and serenely quiet; where she would normally be standing to greet arriving passengers.

Obviously there would be nothing normal about the next twelve days. What an ending for her job on the *Diamond Queen*! That fact hit her with stunning impact as she looked down at the hundreds of fans gathered below on the dock. Men, women and children, short and tall, young and old, were roasting under the relentless Florida sun. And they were getting a bit restless, waiting for the arrival of Michael Shannon, daytime television's answer to Mel Gibson, Kevin Costner, Harrison Ford and Daniel Day Lewis, all rolled into one.

Shannon, as Tamara was beginning to call him in her mind—usually with a slight sniff—alias Stephen Diamond, resident bad boy on *Another Hospital*, currently the highest rated soap opera on television, looked to be a standard Hollywood jerk. Regardless, he was hers to chaperone, pamper and appease for the next twelve days. And there were five *other* cast members, she grimly reminded herself.

Gamely, she plastered a wide smile on her face and started down the gangplank. This was not an auspicious beginning. Shannon was late; in fact, they were all late. The fans waited none too patiently and the newspaper and television people looked expectantly up at her. Everyone wanted action and she had to deliver.

To think, once she had wanted all of this adoration for herself.

She rubbed her fingers over the sudden low ache in her stomach as she swallowed back the painful memories. The price of her dream had been way too high. It had been a difficult battle, but that knowledge no longer made her sad; it made her damn mad! She hadn't given up all she had worked for easily.

Her anger gave her the courage to stroll down the gangplank confidently and, smiling, hold up her hands to the crowd for silence. She ignored the microphone shoved into her face and gave her full attention to the fans until their voices quieted to a low rumble.

"I want to thank you for your patience and apologize for the delay." Her amplified voice trumpeted out over the dock. "I assure you, the cast of *Another Hospital* will be joining us any moment now."

As if on cue, a white stretch limo slowed to a halt at the end of the pier. The crowd cheered and pushed against the police barricades she had ordered as a precaution. A liveried driver jumped out and ran around to open the passenger door with a flourish.

Long, tanned, shapely legs appeared.

A collective groan from the waiting fans was punctuated by a few excited shouts. Then someone yelled,

"Jackie! Jackie!" The name was caught up by others until it became the universal cry.

Even if Tamara hadn't done her homework, she'd have known the beautiful red-haired woman exiting the limo was Jacqueline Evans, the infamous Alexandria of *Another Hospital.* Her expensive white suit hugged every luscious curve of her statuesque body. Her hat alone probably cost about three months' worth of Tamara's salary.

In high heels Jackie Evans must have been nearly six feet tall. At five foot four, Tamara had never felt particularly short; her aerobics classes kept her slim and taut, which created the allusion that she was taller than she actually was. Now suddenly, she felt very small and inconsequential.

Jackie, holding a Louis Vuitton carrying case in each hand, strolled majestically toward the eager crowd. Behind her, the chauffeur struggled with a Vuitton trunk in one hand and two Vuitton suitcases in the other.

Three reporters surged forward, thrusting microphones into Jackie's face. Tamara stepped back from the limelight, checking the proximity of the dock's edge. But Jackie kept advancing, the reporters and a television crew surrounding her with the attention she so obviously adored.

"Darlings, let me catch my breath!" Jackie's low husky laugh brought every male within hearing distance to rigid attention. "Of course, you may take pictures. I think the light will be best right here."

She stopped in front of Tamara and turned around, a wickedly playful smile curving her apricot lips.

Without warning, she thrust her cases forward and Tamara automatically reached for them.

"That's a darling. Hold these for me," she purred.

The cases weighed a ton, pulling on Tamara's arms, but she gripped the leather handles tightly.

"Now, darlings, you may have your fill of me!" Laughing, Jackie swung back toward the cameras, sweeping her arms in a wide arc.

That gesture nearly caught Tamara across the face. Automatically, she jerked away.

She realized her mistake the instant her left heel hit the pier edge. For one heart-stopping moment, she hung suspended in midair. Then the sudden drop wrenched her stomach against her ribs.

In that split second one thought lodged in her brain: She couldn't let these expensive cases sink to the bottom of the bay!

She hit the water with a tremendous splash, the combined weight of the cases dragging her down. *Keep your mouth shut,* instinct demanded as the waves closed over her head. God only knew what was in this murky water!

Adrenaline surged through her, giving her the impetus to struggle upward, still clutching the cases, until she broke the surface. She opened her eyes in time to see a streak diving toward her, and she opened her mouth, taking a long deep gulp of air. Then she sank into the scummy depths for the second time.

Arms encircled her waist. She hadn't been afraid before, assuming the crowd wouldn't just stand there and let her drown, but now panic overtook her. The arms were pulling her down, not to safety!

Without thinking, she began to struggle against the dark shadow with her in the water. But the shadow persevered, grabbing at one of her thrashing arms and gripping her leg. Warm fingers slid between her upper thighs. That intimacy, even in the midst of her panic, sent a shock wave through her. She lifted her knee, making contact hard enough to send the dark shadow away.

She needed air. Her lungs were scalding and felt ready to burst. Using every ounce of her dwindling strength, she kicked upward, once more breaking the surface long enough for a sweet gasp of oxygen.

Again her waist was gripped and for the third time she was plunged back into darkness. What was going on? This guy was supposed to be rescuing her, not drowning her!

GOD, SHE'S GOING TO DROWN us both! Michael Shannon cursed inwardly, his gut aching from her knee jab and every muscle in his body taut as he tried to get a grip on the struggling woman.

One of the heavy cases banged against his bad knee. He cursed silently. What the hell was the matter with this woman?

Then she was gone. For an instant he panicked; how would he ever find her in this underwater world of wavering shadows and murk?

He cut the surface for a fresh breath, then dived deeply until he caught a glimpse of her. With one strong kick he was close enough to grab her again. He reached out and found his hands full of soft breast.

Damn it, it wasn't his fault she kept fighting him! Didn't she understand he was trying to rescue her?

Steeling his muscles to withstand her thrashing body, he wrapped himself around her like a vise and kicked them both upward. They broke the surface at the same time.

"Let go of those damn cases!" he gasped into her face, or at least what he could see of it through the mat of hair plastered across it.

"They're worth a fortune." Her muffled words were hardly decipherable.

He tugged the hair away from her mouth.

"Ouch," she complained, renewing her frantic efforts to free herself from his hold. "Quit trying to drown me!"

His muscles burned from overexertion and her struggling kicks. Frustrated, he tightened his grip and slammed a hard kiss against her parted lips just to shut her up.

She tasted of salt and oil and hair. It shouldn't have been pleasurable at all but an unexpected sweetness curled down his throat.

"Be quiet!" he whispered, sliding his mouth to her ear. "You're the one who's going to drown us. Now, drop those damn cases!"

"Mr. Shannon, grab the life preserver!" A voice calling from above them broke the odd feeling that they were the only two people in the world.

He kept one arm firmly clasped across her breasts and totally disregarded her struggle, pulling her toward the lifeline. Two sailors jumped into the water and helped him lift her to several men who helped her safely onto the dock.

Why in the hell was she still holding on to those cases?

He climbed up behind her. His hair hung in his eyes and his ruined Armani suit clung to him like a second skin. He'd lost both shoes and probably ruined his new wristwatch, which he suddenly remembered *wasn't* waterproof.

That didn't matter; those things could be easily replaced. But what a sideshow he'd given the fans and press!

Brushing aside the cameramen, he moved toward the bedraggled creature he'd just fished out of the Atlantic Ocean. He wanted to see the face that went with that surprisingly sweet mouth.

Drab hair hung in the unattractive lank bunches over her face and a chignon had unrolled at the back of her neck. Her once-white blouse and skirt were streaked with grime and stuck in clumps all over her body.

Gesturing the group hovering around her to move back, he stopped in front of her, careful not to touch her again. "Are you all right?"

At his soft question, her head jerked up and she sucked in a deep breath. Finally dropping the cases in two sodden heaps beside her, she lifted both hands and brushed her hair out of her eyes.

The face she turned up to him was notable if only for the eyes—deep green, spiked by short thick lashes. They glared at him, so he let his gaze wander down to her full lower lip, the source of such bewildering enjoyment, and noticed it veered toward the pouty. So, the young lady obviously had a temper.

"I'm fine. I suppose, thanks to you." Her voice was as cold as the scrutiny she raked over him.

"Darling, but of course, it's thanks to *us* that you've been saved from a watery grave!" Pushing to Tamara's other side, Jackie gushed as only she could. "Gentlemen, get a picture of Michael and me rescuing this poor dear."

To the young woman's credit, she didn't cringe as the cameras clicked away and a member of the television crew stuck a microphone under her nose. No doubt this picture would be splashed on the front page of every supermarket tabloid in the country; Jackie looking like a million bucks, the stranger looking pitiful and him . . . looking all wet.

Jackie was nothing if not predictable.

What *did* surprise him was this young woman's attitude. He expected some gratitude, at least, for fishing her out of the ocean. He sure as hell didn't expect her icy disdain. Who was she? And, more to the point, what did she have against him?

With a tight little smile, she moved slowly toward the gangplank, the media trailing after her.

"God, what great press! I couldn't have arranged this better myself. They got everything! That kiss in the water was a stroke of genius, Mike. It will make every newscast and tabloid in the country!"

Michael stripped off his ruined jacket and glanced at his agent. "Harry, quit acting like my publicist. Just find out that woman's name."

"I already know it. She's Tamara Hayes." He rubbed his hands together in excitement. "I can see the headlines now—Diamond On The *Diamond* Rescues Activities Director In Charge Of Soap Opera Event!"

Remembering the feel of her full breasts and the taste of her mouth, Michael's dread of the next twelve days began to fade. Intrigued with this new possibility for pleasure, he smiled up at her as he watched her make her way onto the ship, dripping a watery trail behind her.

"Send a dozen pink roses to her cabin. No, make it two dozen." He threw the words back over his shoulder as he followed her aboard.

Recognizing his duty to his fans, he stopped long enough to wave and smile at the crowd. They cheered in response. He left Jackie holding court and went straight to his stateroom. He'd make it up to the fans at the bon voyage party by staying beyond his prescribed time and signing all the autographs they wanted. But just now, he needed a long hot shower to wash off the grime and the smell of diesel fuel that had permeated the water.

He left his ruined clothes in a heap on the floor of the tiny bathroom and stepped under the shower. Turning the faucets as hot and high as they would go, he let the water beat on his head and down over his shoulders and back. His muscles were still tense from his watery dance with Tamara Hayes.

What a beginning! He hadn't wanted to do this promotional cruise in the first place. He *shouldn't* have done it, considering what he planned to do when he got back; but he owed Harry and Harry wanted it.

Now he was out his favorite suit and his handmade Italian shoes. Plus he would have to deal with the belligerent woman whose life he'd just saved, and who, he had a sneaking suspicion, was probably in charge of all the cast-fan activities for the duration of the cruise.

He turned off the hot water and reached for a towel, remembering Harry's words. Agents were always quick to turn everything to advantage, he thought ruefully. But maybe that kiss *had* been pure genius. Maybe hitting on the uptight but tasty Miss Hayes might alleviate some of the problems he foresaw brewing on this trip. He laughed out loud, the sound echoing in the tiny tiled shower stall. That little scene he'd played had all the makings of a plot straight out of *Another Hospital!* All it needed was the proverbial other man or woman to really spice it up.

Jackie was waiting for him in his cabin when he stepped out of the bathroom, a white towel slung loosely around his hips. Posed seductively across his bed, she blinked up at him from her magnificent heavy-lidded eyes and smiled her come-hither smile.

"How did you get in here?" he asked, recognizing too well the look on her face.

"I told your stewardess we had an engagement, so she let me in." Stretching so her breasts were clearly defined against her jacket, Jackie stood. "She watches the show and hopes we get back together after our last messy divorce. So do I, of course. We're always better when we're together."

In her stockinged feet Jackie came only to his chin. She leaned toward him, and the top button of her suit jacket opened, exposing the deep V between her breasts. "Darling, why are you clutching that towel so tightly? It isn't as if I haven't seen it all before."

He stopped her hand at the edge of the terry cloth and circled her wrist with tight fingers. "That was a long time ago, Jackie. The cameras aren't rolling now. You're Jacqueline Evans, not Alexandria."

"But, darling, this *is* me." She rubbed against him seductively, her breasts pressing into his bare chest. "Just as Stephen Diamond is a part of you. That's what's so fascinating about you now. Michael Shannon is as wickedly enticing as his alter ego."

Her words were like cold water dripping over his damp bare flesh. They made him remember that icy look Tamara Hayes had given him. He found it hard to admit, even to himself, how much he'd come to live his on-camera role offscreen, as well.

And reviewing today's events, he realized he was planning to keep living his role a while longer.

He didn't like the feeling that gave him. Stephen Diamond might be sexy and unprincipled, but he'd always thought better of himself. This only reinforced his desire to get out.

"What do you want, Jackie?" he asked slowly, peering down at her smooth, elaborately made-up face.

She laughed deep in her throat. "Why, isn't it obvious, darling? I want you. Right now."

A quick tattoo on the door was followed by the latch clicking and the door opening. Jackie jumped away from him, cursing, "I should have locked the damn thing!" A white line of anger showed around her moist lips.

Michael couldn't help sighing with relief. He was in no mood for her tricks. He'd be fighting her off the entire trip, he supposed. *Unless he carried through with his plan.*

Harry pushed the door open and entered, carrying a bottle of scotch. All the color drained from his ruddy complexion. "God, I'm sorry. I'll come back later."

"Don't bother, Harry. Come on it. Jackie was just leaving," Michael insisted.

Jackie slid him one long speculative look before shrugging with a resigned little sigh. "As a matter of fact, I should be leaving. We mustn't keep our loyal fans waiting."

She slipped into her discarded high heels and glided through the open door. "See you poolside, my darlings." Blowing kisses, she disappeared down the hall.

"What is she up to?" he asked. "And lock that damn door so I don't have any more interruptions!"

Michael didn't have much time to get ready so he took a slug right out of the bottle. While Harry silently leaned back against the door, Michael moved around the room, digging underwear, slacks and a polo shirt out of his suitcase. He threw his towel to the floor and finished dressing. He and Harry had been roommates years ago when he'd first gone to L.A. straight out of Northwestern University, a headstrong kid, anxious to make his mark in the world of film. They had no secrets.

At Harry's continued silence, Michael looked around. "What gives? Jackie's your client, too.... Anything going on I should know about?"

Shaking his head, Harry said, "I delivered your roses myself."

Michael studied his friend's carefully composed face. "And?"

"She was civil, even told me to thank you. And from what I could see before she shut the door in my face, our little Miss Hayes cleans up real good."

REAL GOOD—Harry should be hanged! She was a knockout. From the gorgeous wheat-blond hair hanging in waves to her waist, to huge slanted cat eyes, to the body that he knew by touch was firm and rounded in all the right places, even though the cruise uniform she was wearing hid her figure.

Remembering again the feel and taste of her, Michael waited off to one side of the pool deck and watched Tamara do her job. She controlled the anxious fans and introduced the cast: Linn Bass and Wayne Weston, who played the young misunderstood lovers, Bonnie and Bill, went first. Then came Tracy Adams, the heart and conscience of *Another Hospital,* Grandma Lily. The fans roared their approval as Jackie stepped forward into the limelight.

There was a short pause, and the crowd surged forward, but Tamara raised her hand for order, introducing Sheila Peterson, the show's new associate producer. Some of her innovations had received mixed reaction from the fans, but these remained polite, if not enthusiastic. Just as the crowd was becoming restless again, Michael moved so Tamara could see him.

He took a deep breath as she announced, "And now, the moment you've all been waiting for..."

To this day, he didn't understand the fan reaction, but he found he was actually beginning to take it for granted.

"As one fan magazine put it, here's the man you love to hate. Stephen Diamond himself, Michael Shannon!"

What the hell kind of an introduction was that?

The words were properly enthusiastic and her smile looked totally convincing, unless you stared into her deep green eyes as he did when he took the microphone from her. Deliberately he brushed his fingers across hers. Her eyes widened a little, flashing with frost, although the expression on her heart-shaped face never altered an inch, maintaining her lovely smile.

For a moment, her strange reaction sent a streak of shock along his nerves, arousing a predatory instinct he'd thought long gone. The challenge to conquer this young woman suddenly burned like liquid fire in his veins.

God! He was getting as jaded as his character.

But he couldn't seem to let go of the idea all through his carefully rehearsed patter. And, he rationalized, his pursuit of the enigmatic Tamara would keep Jackie at bay for the duration of the cruise.

Holding that thought, he returned the microphone to her with a melting look. She turned her back on him. Or did she?

She was good, he had to give her that. She made it seem as if she'd turned away to field questions from the fans, but he saw the rejection in her eyes.

She pushed the microphone back in his face and he realized he'd just been asked a question. He'd have to stop thinking about her and start interacting with the fans. They'd paid good money to spend the next twelve days with "the Diamond," and he was determined to give them their money's worth.

The cast answered questions for over an hour, although most were directed at him. After giving autographs for another forty-five minutes, his cast mates deserted him. A half hour later, a line still stretched around the deck, adoring fans waiting patiently for his autographs.

His hand cramping, he decided he's sell his soul for another scotch, but he kept at it. He noticed Tamara had stayed with him, diplomatically moving zealous fans away when they got too pushy and making sure each passenger had the same amount of time with him.

As long as she stayed, he would, too.

He always delivered what he promised. Shaking out his fingers, he looked down the line of waiting fans, noticing some faces back for the second time. But Tamara was a quick study. Realizing what was happening, she went straight to the microphone.

"Ladies and gentlemen, you'll have many more opportunities in the days ahead to visit with your favorite characters. That's all for now. The bell for the first seating at dinner will sound in a few minutes and I know you'll all want to get ready for the rest of tonight's activities."

"One more question, Michael!" a voice from the back persisted. "Who kissed Tamara? Was it Michael Shannon for good press? Or was it Stephen Diamond and just for the hell of it?"

He settled his eyes firmly on Tamara's face. An enchanting blush turned her skin pink, although she remained resolutely at the microphone.

He lifted his lips in a half smile and strolled over to her.

"Stephen and Michael always get exactly what they want. Today they want Miss Hayes."

Then, before she could escape, he bent toward her. The crowd chuckled, satisfied, but he never completed the kiss, just turned off the microphone and whispered to her, "Can I talk to you alone for a minute?"

He would find the reason behind that icy look no matter what it took, and he would melt it. Beneath her loose-fitting jacket he could see her shoulders stiffen.

"Mr. Shannon, I may be your escort for the next twelve days, but I'd appreciate it if you didn't make me a part of your little PR stunts."

The words were as cool and crisp as her brittle smile. Was she angry because he'd kissed her, or because she thought he had staged it?

By the set of her delicate chin, Michael could tell she was well-armored against his next salvo. Yet the challenge was irresistible.

Patience remained one of his few lingering virtues; he would pick the place and the moment for seduction. For now, he would be cautious.

"Tamara, I just wanted to make sure you're fully recovered from our dip together." Capturing one of her hands, he gave her a smile calculated to charm. "I can see your fingers are bruised. Why wouldn't you let go of those damn cases of Jackie's today?"

Her lashes flickered upward in surprise and a pang of pleasure settled in his chest. But that's all he got. She slid her hand free and favored him with another cool glance. Miss Hayes wasn't about to be charmed by the likes of him.

"I don't really know. I just latched on to them for dear life. Not letting those cases sink to the muddy bottom, even though they weighed a ton, seemed very important at the time." Something shifted in her green eyes as she shook her head. "What does she carry in them?"

"All her beauty aids," he stated baldly. His words had been aiming for one response and he got it. She couldn't quite hide a quivering smile before she rushed away.

Out of nowhere, somewhat like her character on the show, Tracy appeared, a deep frown slashed between her knowing eyes.

"Oh, no, I've seen that look before!" he said as he draped an arm across Tracy's shoulders affectionately. "What have I done now?"

"It's not what you've done—it's what you're thinking of doing. I've seen that wolfish gleam in your eyes often enough to know what happens next!" She gave him her "Grandma Lily" stare of reproach. "That's a nice girl there. Don't you be working the Stephen Diamond line on that young pretty thing."

"Don't worry." He pressed a kiss on the older woman's forehead beneath the fringe of white bangs. Tracy was a real friend and one he could trust. "I'll be very careful around her."

"CAREFUL! 'I'll be very careful around her,'" Jackie mimicked. "Why should he treat her differently than any of the others?" she fumed before taking a long drag on a cigarette, just to settle her nerves. She coughed and flung it into the ocean in disgust. "I can't believe he's actually interested in that skinny little brat."

"You told me you gave up smoking." Harry leaned on the ship's railing, peering at her with worried blue eyes.

"Quit nagging! I threw the thing away, didn't I? And I'll throw that little brat into the ocean, too, before I let her spoil my plans for Michael!"

"You already did once."

The memory of how truly dreadful the younger woman had looked after Michael fished her out of the water engendered total delight. She could hardly wait to see the pictures in all the papers. She'd be sure to send a copy to Tamara's cabin the minute she got her hands on them.

Slightly mollified, she ran one finger down Harry's ruddy cheek. "Harry, darling, you will help me, won't you?"

"I got Michael on this boat for you, Jackie," he answered with no intonation in his voice. "What more do you want?"

Lowering her lids to mere slits, she brushed her lips over his cheek. "Why, darling, I only want you to get me exactly what I want—just like always."

Day Two—At Sea

Tamara ran the last few yards to the area in front of the sun deck gym where she taught her 6:00 a.m. aerobics class. Her boom box bumped against her side and pulled on her sore right arm, a reminder of yesterday's fiasco with Shannon.

Six women waited for her, and three of them were from the soap opera. Jackie shot her a look of pure loathing, then tried to mask it with a friendly wave. Tamara blinked with surprise. Had she just imagined that blistering glare? She'd thought Jackie a better actress than that. Unless she *wanted* Tamara to know they had not hit it off.

For a moment, dismay curled in her stomach. Then, trying to ignore Jackie, she smiled brightly at the other exercise enthusiasts: Florence from California, who was holding an avid conversation with Tracy; and two young women, Shirley and Eileen from Ohio, both of whom she vaguely remembered seeing the night before. Linn stood off to one side, not making any effort to join the group.

"Good morning, ladies. Let's start to burn that fat!" She refused to deal with personalities this early in the morning, especially after a night filled with dreams of Shannon's hands holding her breasts and his fingers slipping between her thighs and his mouth bruising her lips over and over again. Shivering slightly at the memories, she flipped on the exercise tape and immediately threw herself into her routine.

"Now let's warm up. Touch those toes!" she encouraged over the rock music pounding across the deck.

She had to give the two older women a lot of credit. Tracy and Florence valiantly kept pace even after she moved the group into more energetic jazz steps. Jackie and Linn were both obvious exercise pros—they couldn't keep those bodies without constant workouts. Tamara wasn't surprised. She knew how important the body beautiful was in Hollywood.

What did surprise her was Jackie's attitude. She constantly positioned herself in front of the large glass windows that made up one wall of the gym. *Now if it were a mirror...*

Curious, Tamara maneuvered the routine around, turning her back to the class so she could peer through the glass into the gym beyond to see what Jackie found so intriguing.

Her eyes locked with Michael Shannon's. He stood with a weighted barbell in his hands, watching her with a fascinated grin. Or was he watching Jackie? He winked before finishing a military press over his head. A wave of thick black hair fell across his eyes and Tamara turned sharply away, dismay replaced by something entirely different in the pit of her stomach.

For the first time, she realized how sexual exercise could seem. Except for sport bras and strips of span-

dex, she and the younger women were practically naked. They thrust out their breasts and gyrated their
hips to the music, throwing themselves mentally as
well as physically into the movements.

Knowing Shannon was watching made her skin
burn, but she resolved her steps wouldn't falter. Tomorrow morning, however, she'd wear a nonreveal-
ing sweat suit like the ones Florence and Tracy were
wearing.

Suddenly, she remembered what came next. A jazzy
step would turn her back toward the window and keep
her looking that way for the rest of the routine. Maybe
he'd be gone. Maybe he'd...

Darn the man! Hands on hips, beatific smile
planted on the perfect planes of his face, he stood
watching, without even the pretence of weights in
hand.

She tripped over her left foot. Somehow she turned
the stumble into a swinging move and turned back to
the class. Enough was enough!

"Okay, ladies, let's call it a day," she shouted and
abruptly switched off the tape. The sudden quiet
seemed oddly jarring in the early-morning mist.

"I thought this was an hour class." Jackie stretched
and glanced at her Rolex. "We've only been at it for
thirty minutes. I want my full class time."

"Tamara is taking pity on Florence and me," Tracy
cut in, giving Jackie a pointed look before glancing
back to Tamara. "Thanks, hon, it felt good."

Tracy's smile was pure "Grandma Lilly," but her
voice sounded so much earthier that when she was in
character that Tamara couldn't help but grin back at
her.

"Yeah, thanks," Linn called absently before racing to catch up with Wayne, who was just walking out the other door with Shannon.

Michael propped one shoulder against the outside window, leering at her like a tomcat eyeing his dinner. Except *he* was the rat!

"Oh...look at that body!" The whispered gush came from Eileen, right behind her and loud enough to hear all the way along the deck.

"And that face! He just makes me melt," Shirley added. "Don't you think he's gorgeous, Tamara?"

Their rapt adoration seemed so simple and innocent. Probably as innocent as she and Allison had been when they'd first arrived in L.A. For some reason, all those memories seemed very close and very painful. She thought she'd gotten over them a long time ago. Suddenly, she couldn't prevent a prickling of tears behind her eyes and whirled as much to warn the two young women that voices carried on the water as to cover her own melancholy.

Damn! She couldn't help Ally now, but she could sure try to nip this naive adoration in the bud. Men like Michael Shannon didn't need it. Or deserve it.

"Oh, I don't know." She shrugged, nonchalantly draping a towel around her damp neck. "There are two pharmacists from Cleveland with the drugstore tour who are just as good-looking. I'll introduce them to you tonight. *Real* men are so much more fascinating, don't you think?"

She'd expected some reaction but certainly not the round-eyed looks of horror transforming both their pretty faces.

"Good morning, ladies." Shannon's purr came from directly behind her.

She whipped around, her breasts brushing his chest where a band of tanned flesh showed between his black cutoff sweatshirt and nylon running shorts. The glint in his ebony eyes left no doubt he'd heard every word she'd said. She took two quick steps back, away from him.

"Would you mind if I have a word with Tamara alone?" he asked, throwing a lazy smile between the two young women as he took one step forward to tower over her. "I hope I'll see you both tonight at the cocktail party."

"We'll be there!" they gasped in unison.

"Don't forget," Tamara said, lifting her chin before turning back to them, "I'll make those introductions tonight."

Nodding, they rushed off, no doubt full of gossip to share with the rest of the "Diamond on Diamond" group. Rumors of trouble between her and Shannon would make her job a bit harder to handle, but not as difficult as what she had to face right now.

He devoured her workout clothes with a wolfish gleam in his eye. Until this morning, she'd never thought the outfit too skimpy or revealing.

"About your job." His words so matched her thoughts that she blinked up at him in surprise. "I'd like to talk to you over lunch about the schedule of events on board."

Instantly on her guard, which obviously she'd have to maintain this whole miserable trip, she shook her head. "You received a list of—"

"Mr. Shannon! Mr. Shannon!" A tiny gray-haired woman rushed up and interrupted her by grabbing Michael's hand. "I'm Irma Wright and this is my husband, Joe, and we're just your biggest fans! We're going to videotape every minute of 'Diamond on Diamond'! I'm the president of your fan club back in Omaha and I promised the girls I'd record everything!"

With her other hand, she waved at her husband. "Farther back, Joe! I want the whole deck *and* the smokestack in the picture."

Video camera to his eye, Joe Wright backed away, leaning dangerously over the railing, tottering on tiptoe, looking ready to lose his footing at any second.

Instinctively, Tamara stepped toward him, but Shannon was ahead of her, having somehow extricated himself from Irma's iron grip.

"Joe, may I offer a suggestion?" In one swift movement, he had the older man steady on his feet again, and led him away from danger. "Although I studied theater arts at Northwestern University, I took some film courses." He dropped his voice to a collaborative tone. "You'll get a much better shot if you study the contrast of light and shadows. Say, over there by the smokestack, and then you could pan the whole deck and get in some of the view."

Irma hurried over to them, anxious not to miss a thing.

Without warning, Jackie appeared from around the corner. "He's quite something, isn't he, darling?" she murmured into Tamara's ear, her moist apricot lips curled into a predatory smile. "And for your information he's *all* mine."

The blaze in her eyes practically scorched Tamara's face before the actress strutted off across the deck. Tamara wasn't sure if her exit was for Joe's camera or to impress Shannon. She only knew Jackie had managed to make her blood boil.

Her veiled threat was too reminiscent of the days Tamara had spent in L.A.—working so hard to follow her dream, before watching it all turn to dust. Anger blocked her common sense when it came to Shannon. She hadn't played the game all those years ago and she sure as heck wasn't going to play it now! Not with Shannon, not with anyone!

Deliberately, she waited for him to finish charming the socks off Joe and Irma. Might as well get this over with as soon as possible, she thought.

He strolled lazily back to her. His cutoff sweatshirt showed every rippling muscle of his stomach and the too-brief nylon shorts left no doubt to his masculinity.

"About that talk," she blurted out before he could say anything. "Let's get something straight. I know there's no substitute for good press, but you had your fun yesterday." Try as she might, she couldn't help glaring at him. "I suggest you find someone else to make Jackie jealous. I'm not available."

Had he practiced the way his absurdly thick lashes fluttered over his eyes when his lips curled in that enticing, come-hither smile? Given enough time, this man could probably wring a response from a stone. Despite the barriers she'd built up, she had to admit he had an effect on her. A small ache spread downward from the pit of her stomach.

Even his shrug looked sexy. "The kiss was no PR stunt and it sure as hell didn't have anything to do with Jackie. It just happened, Tamara. So did my interest in you. Why are you afraid of honest attraction?"

Feeling suddenly hot and flustered, she searched for an appropriate response. If she had to be at this man's beck and call for the next eleven days because of her job, she needed to seize control of the situation, and right now!

Drawing on her sense of duty, she threw him what she hoped was a mask of professional politeness, and bent to pick up her boom box.

"You're a professional and so am I. Tonight, and in the future, Mr. Shannon, please afford me the professional courtesy I deserve. I don't enjoy playing games."

He shifted his body, blocking her escape route. A light—or was it a small flame?—shone in his ebony eyes, and he stood so close to her, she inhaled the tangy scent of his after-shave. Suddenly, he seemed overpowering; her little defenses would be no match for him. Fear shot through her bloodstream.

"Why are you afraid of me, Tamara? You don't know me yet. Give me a chance." He reached out to touch her arm.

She jumped back as if he'd singed her.

Shock widened his eyes and he stepped away, flinging his arms wide in a frustrated arc.

On one level she recognized she was overreacting. But she'd joined the staff on the *Diamond Queen* to get away from L.A.—to rebuild her life. She'd done that, at least she thought she had. She just didn't need any reminder of that old life.

Swallowing, she forced a smile. "Sorry. You took me by surprise."

"No. I'm sorry." Slowly, his eyes searched her face. "For some reason, we've gotten off to a rough start. I'd like to talk about it. How about tonight?"

His request, spoken so gently, could only be answered in kind. "Okay. We'll talk tonight," she agreed before sliding sideways past him.

She made her escape, feeling his eyes burn into her spine until she could get out of sight. Why now, on her last cruise, did the past have to catch up with her?

NONE TOO PATIENTLY, Michael had anticipated this moment all day. He stood in the wings of the small stage in the show lounge watching Tamara. She was really good at what she did, talking to the crowd, building their anticipation without a lot of hype.

It always amazed him that anyone showed up to ask a few questions or get an autograph or maybe just see the cast of the show.

Or to see. He couldn't forget that. Wasn't that why he didn't carry out his threat to go for broke with his dream? He couldn't give up the applause; the kick-in-the-gut thrill he got from performing. But somehow, that conflict had been totally forgotten today. He'd been thinking about Tamara. She was quite an enigma. Her appearance said one thing, but her actions said another.

Take tonight. Luxuriant pale gold hair hung down her back and fell over her shoulders so he couldn't tell where it ended and the form-fitting gold sequin gown she wore began. From where he stood, she glowed in the dim light. But was she using her sex appeal to her own advantage? Not as far as he could tell.

At the moment, she was introducing the two star-struck women from the exercise class to two young men, just as she'd promised. She didn't seem to want every man in the room to look at her, like most of the women he'd come in contact with the past few years. And yet, somehow, he couldn't take his eyes off her.

The women he'd met in Hollywood had all seemed to love him—or to want to use him. Why did this woman act as though he was poison?

He'd heard every word she'd said that morning and was more intrigued than insulted by her comments. Something, or someone, had definitely soured her on men. He would also discover the answer to that before he was finished.

Harry rushed up, a worried look on his face. "Mike, I've got to have your answer. C'mon, pal, I'm counting on you!"

Perspiration beaded his lined forehead and the bleak gaze demanded some response. Michael studied his agent, his friend. They'd always been straightforward with each other, from the very beginning of their friendship, even before the professional relationship had formed.

"What's wrong, Harry? You look like hell."

"What's wrong?" Harry shrugged his shoulders and fiddled with the top button of his tux shirt. "I lost two clients to other agencies last week. The overhead in my office is killing me. And you insist on playing hardball with the network! What could be wrong?" A ghost of his old devil-may-care smile flickered briefly. "C'mon, Mike, sign the new three-year contract with the show. It will make us both a lot richer. And your fans will be happy."

He looked over Harry's shoulder at the room filled with those fans. At times like this, when everything was going well, he couldn't deny he was tempted. After all, saying yes was a safe decision; but something, some intangible nagged at him.

"I haven't made up my mind yet. I need more time."

"Time!" Harry thrust his flushed face closer. "The time is now, pal! I've got Sheila Peterson right here. I can clinch the deal. We can make the announcement here, during the cruise. Wouldn't that be a coup?"

"Don't push, Harry. I'll decide in a few days." He relented more out of concern for his friend's pained expression than any real desire to make the decision. "Curtain's going up."

Harry pushed his way through the rest of the cast who had been assembling for several minutes. Jackie arrived just as Tamara moved toward the microphone, her usual ploy. He didn't know how Jackie did it, but her sense of timing was impeccable. He'd seen her show up on the set on her day off, just because someone from the press had arrived unexpectedly. She must have some kind of radar.

Tamara turned toward him, to check if everyone was present, and a hot stab of desire pierced his gut, taking his mind off everything except her. In that dress Tamara took his breath away. He stood gazing at her, his mind imagining sliding those spaghetti straps off her shoulders and peeling the clinging fabric down over her breasts. At the very least, he wanted to place his flat palm low on her back where creamy flesh met sequins.

He couldn't take his eyes off her.

"Poor darling, what an unfortunate choice of dress." Jackie curled her hand around his arm, tapping one long red nail against his sleeve. "Those sequins are merciless, you know. So young and already she needs a tummy tuck."

"Pull in your claws, Jackie," Tracy sneered from behind him. "All this envy is making lines in your forehead."

Instantly, a compact mirror flashed in Jackie's hand and she surveyed her flawless skin. After the briefest glance, she snapped it shut and looked up.

"Tracy, darling, I forgot to tell you the latest gossip," she cooed maliciously. "The powers-that-be think it's time old Grandma Lily plays her death scene."

If he'd learned anything in his fifteen years in the business, it was to stay out of feuds between actors—unless it looked like it was going to turn into a cat fight. He shifted his body between Jackie and Tracy.

"Hey, gang, here we go!" Wayne's stage whisper brought everyone to attention.

Linn took Wayne's hand and together they ran out onto the stage. Michael frowned. They seemed to be doing that more and more lately, which was not good for their careers. After a while, people would think of them as a permanent team. He'd have to speak to them.

After a burst of applause, Tracy followed. There was a roar of approval—everyone loved Grandma Lily, both offstage and on.

Jackie flung her shoulders back, thrust her magnificent breasts out and wiggled seductively into the limelight. They were all pros—the show would go on no matter what happened backstage. There was another roar of approval, and Michael just waited for her to get her full due.

Then without missing a beat, he joined the others so they could all hold hands and bow on cue.

While they performed, Tamara stayed in the shadows. He could feel her watching him and the anticipation that had been growing for hours turned into an almost physical ache. He hadn't felt excitement for the chase in a very long time. He'd had enough heartache to last a lifetime. That seemed to be one of the reasons he'd just concentrated on getting the job done for the last year, anticipating the end of his contract.

Now Harry was pressuring him to renew. Maybe that's why all the old doubts were surfacing to confuse him.

Absorbed in his thoughts, he was caught off guard when Jackie latched on to his arm and refused to let go. Even when they all stepped offstage to mingle, she stuck to his side as if she'd been glued there.

The fans expected them to be a twosome after eight years on the show. Their characters had bedded each other countless times, and cheated on each other even more often—before, during and after their five engagements and two marriages, which were always rapidly followed by messy divorces. The public never seemed to tire of Stephen and Alexandria.

He knew Sheila was writing one more reunion for their characters, saying the fans were clamoring for it. So tonight he would let Jackie monopolize him and give them what they wanted, for the sake of good public relations. But that didn't prevent him from keeping a close eye on Tamara; he never lost sight of her or stayed too far out of earshot.

Right now she was keeping an anxious eye on the video-camera twins, Irma and Joe, after Tracy nearly fell over them as they scuttled around the edge of the small dance floor to capture Linn and Wayne waltzing.

The band struck up a limbo tune. Jackie shuddered and pulled him toward a corner. He watched Tamara secure Joe an excellent vantage point for taping, then turn to make sure the rest of the group was having a good time. At one point, she appeared to sigh, then glanced around with a guilty expression.

At that moment, she caught him watching her from across the room. She blushed. The slow burn traveled from her cheeks down her arms. He found himself contemplating how her skin would feel against his, especially when she looked so delectable.

He lifted Jackie's hand to his lips and pressed a quick kiss on her fingers. "See you later." He ignored the sharp scrape of her nails along his skin, putting as much distance between them as possible before he threw a smile at a fan converging on him. "Will you please excuse me?"

His sight was set on only one objective. He lifted two champagne glasses from a passing waiter's tray and headed straight for her.

She realized his intent an instant too late to escape. Joe stood on her right and the crowded limbo floor on her left. Behind her the crowd clapped enthusiastically.

"This is for you," he purred, handing her the icy champagne glass. "Because you've been working so hard."

Her eyes shot green flames at him over the glass rim. "What do you want, Mr. Shannon? I thought I made myself clear this morning."

"Crystal clear." He lifted his glass in salute and held it in place until she had to drink from hers. Then, before she could make a recovery, he pried the glass out of her fingers and handed it to Joe.

If he knew anything about women, this would be one of his few chances to get close to her. The orchestra began a slow pulsing tango as the dance floor cleared. Its timing couldn't have been better.

"Dance with me, Tamara."

He could read the rejection in her eyes, but she was caught. A scene would be undignified, as well as unprofessional. And when Jackie started toward him from the corner, Tamara stepped into his arms, perhaps just to thwart her. No matter, she was where he wanted, even if she held herself stiffly away from his encircling arms.

He was a good dancer, but she followed his lead like a professional, making him even better. After a few turns around the floor, her instincts betrayed her and he was able to fit their bodies together like pieces of a puzzle. They moved as one, totally in sync, as if they had been dancing together their whole lives.

His gut twisted in a knot as he discovered she wasn't wearing anything under her gown. Involuntarily his thighs tightened. The contour of her breasts pressed against his chest as their hips thrust together with the slow disciplined movements of the dance, exciting him almost to the point of pain.

Each step she took was graceful and controlled. When he twirled her out, she came willingly back to his arms, even though she glared defiance into his eyes.

That defiance fed the flames licking at him. God, he wanted her!

She flung her head back as he bent her over his arm when the music ended with a flourish. Unable to resist, he leaned over to taste the flushed skin of her throat. It possessed the same sweetness as her mouth.

Thunderous applause echoed around him. For one split second he'd forgotten where he was, who he was. Ever the consummate performer, he lifted her in his arms and twirled her around to the crowd's delight. Then he set her on her feet.

The moment he let her go, she escaped, disappearing into the crowd.

He turned to follow her but at the doorway Harry stopped him.

"Mike, what a performance! Sheila's salivating. C'mon, pal, let's go make her happy."

"Not now, Harry!" The excitement pounding through his blood made his voice sharper than he'd intended.

Harry swayed slightly, sneering, "On the prowl tonight, Mike?"

That wasn't Harry's usual style. "Go to bed, Harry, you're drunk. We'll talk when I'm ready and not before." He shrugged past his friend.

A warm ocean breeze wrapped around him and moonlight lit the deck. Tamara was out here, somewhere in the darkness. And nothing was going to stop him from finding her.

TAMARA GLANCED BACK at the door to the show lounge before she turned the corner. It was still closed, thank heaven. Why had she let him catch her off guard? Why hadn't she crippled him by tripping all over his feet?

No, she'd been too smart for that! She'd just melted into his body and danced as though she had known him forever. She couldn't believe how well their steps had matched, how instinctively their bodies had found a rhythm; almost as if they were one person.

She rubbed her hands down her body, trying to rid it of his touch, his scent. Two years in Hollywood fending off the advances of balding, married casting directors and ambitious young actors with egos and libidos larger than the Caribbean Sea should have taught her a lesson. If not that, certainly her own well-developed sense of self-preservation should have warned her away.

Michael Shannon, soap opera superstar, was dangerous, on and off the stage. She'd recognized that fact the instant he'd touched her; even in the scummy water before she knew who and what he was. After tonight, she realized he wasn't just dangerous, he was lethal.

She paced along the teak deck, putting as much space between herself and him as possible. The peace and quiet of the Caribbean night was strangely soothing and soon she calmed enough to realize she was assigning far too much significance to a tiny episode no one else would even have noticed. She took a deep breath and stopped. The waves splashed against the ship's hull as the *Diamond Queen* sailed directly in line with the moon's path of shimmering light. She lifted her face, closing her eyes, wishing for...she didn't know what.

She began walking again, trailing her fingers lightly along the ship's railing. If Michael Shannon dared to come after her, she was ready. She'd had enough time to reinforce her defenses—all she had to do was think of Ally.

The sight of a man and woman entwined in a passionate embrace brought her to an abrupt standstill. Not wishing to intrude on their privacy, she backed up two steps. Perhaps a board had creaked or she'd made an involuntary sound, for suddenly they broke apart.

In the moonlight, their faces were clearly recognizable: the young couple from the show.

Wayne wrapped a protective arm around Linn's shoulders. "Tamara, please don't say anything to anyone. You could get us into real hot water with the brass."

"She won't say anything, and neither will I. But, damn it, Wayne, you know better!" Michael said from directly behind Tamara. The man must move like a cat! This was the second time he'd been able to sneak up on her. Where had he come from?

Wayne's shoulders slumped in relief. "Thanks, Mike. I knew I could count on you."

"And thank you, Tamara," Linn whispered over her shoulder as her costar dragged her away.

"They must think they're in love." A deadly sensual smile curled Shannon's mouth as he propped himself against the railing beside her.

"Then what's the big deal?" This was good, a red herring that would keep him from the real reason he'd pursued her out into the night.

"The producers frown on offstage relationships between their actors. They think it muddies up the water, that there's all hell to pay when the blowup comes, as it inevitably does."

"Cynic. Maybe it's real for them and won't end." She tightened her grip on the railing, trying to calm her pulse pounding out of control. Why was she so nervous? They were having a conversation, not a sparring match. "Besides, it's an unfair rule. Lots of people fall in love on the job."

He shrugged. "Everything ends one way or another, Tamara. But you're right about it being unfair. For which poor Wayne has me to blame. That rule came down from the brass after Jackie and I blew up five years ago."

Cool silver moonlight etched the perfection of bone knit to bone that was his face. It was too dark to read his ebony eyes, but his voice held a ring of sincerity.

"Excuse me, but I thought you and Jackie were—" she struggled to come up with a polite name for what the tabloids had labeled their relationship "—an item."

"We used to be a PR man's dream. And believe me, Harry took full advantage of it. Still tries to. But now it's all just press hype."

Tamara looked out at the moonlight and explored the predicament her job had propelled her into, willy-nilly. Beyond a shadow of a doubt, she knew the soap opera diva was up to no good—and this man, brains and brawn and body aside, was clueless. That perception suddenly made him seem vulnerable and, regrettably, infinitely more desirable.

Scratch that, she commanded herself; he was already too desirable for anyone's good. Carefully she inched—imperceptibly, she hoped—away from him.

"But I didn't come out here to talk about the show. I came to talk about us. Somehow we got off on the wrong foot. I want to rectify that, if you'll let me."

Not for one instant did she forget he was an actor. And a very good one. His voice, the intent way his eyes searched her face, was utterly convincing. Compared to this performance, Jackie looked amateurish.

In vain, she reminded herself that guys like this were a dime a dozen in show biz. Then her innate honesty rose to protest; very few men possessed what Shannon did—blatant sexuality tempered with an unconscious air of believability.

She felt herself being drawn in—like a moth to a flame, like a deer caught in headlights, like a snake charmer's...

"I don't trust you."

A hot rush of embarrassment burned her cheeks and settled in a solid lump in her stomach. She chewed on her lip. How could she have been so foolish? She was responsible for this man on this trip; she just couldn't blurt out the truth like this... or could she?

She might as well end this foolishness here and now. It would get Jackie off her back and nip in the bud this inconceivable fascination she was beginning to feel for Shannon.

"I'm not into shipboard romances, no matter how tempting. In fact, I'm not into *any* romance, on or off the ship, with a Hollywood bad boy. Your reputation has preceded you, Mr. Shannon, and so far you're living right up to it.''

''Fair enough.''

She let go of some of the tension building up inside. He **was** going to be reasonable.

No, he wasn't.

In one fluid motion, he turned and trapped her against the railing. ''But you did say tempting, didn't you?'' he taunted. ''That sounds downright promising.''

Suddenly, notwithstanding the open air, Tamara found it hard to breathe. Despite her determination to be rid of him, his words conjured up an excitement she couldn't deny. She looked up at him, afraid to say anything else.

He stepped back, giving her some space. ''Let's take it one step, one moment, one day at a time. All I ask is a chance for us to get to know each other better. No hype. Just Tamara and Michael. Then maybe you'll tell me what you're so afraid of.''

She was tough, but she would have had to be made of titanium to resist his potent combination of drop-dead good looks and total sincerity. Finally, she sighed.

''Okay.'' Realizing how weak her voice sounded, she cleared her throat. ''You've got a deal. After all, we will be thrown together a lot in the next few days. Let's make it as painless as possible. Friends?''

She thrust out her hand and inadvertently brushed against his tux shirt. Even though he immediately captured her fingers in his, she'd felt the warmth and strength of his chest through his fine cotton shirt in those few seconds. Her fingers tingled with the contact; and so did her body, remembering the extravagant tango they'd danced together a short while ago.

"Friends." He smiled into her eyes. "It's a beginning. Good night, Tamara." His lips brushed her cheek.

Shock waves exploded along her nerve endings. Could he hear the pounding of her heart? Could he see the flush on her face? Could he feel the heat rushing over her body?

If he'd come on like gangbusters, grabbing her or trying to thrust his tongue into her mouth in a parody of passion, she would have known exactly how to deal with him. But this? This wasn't fair.

She watched him walk away, hands thrust into his trouser pockets, a little swing in his step. She closed her eyes and took a deep breath of bracing salt air. She'd thought she was smarter than this. To fight her sudden lack of good sense, she called up the old painful memories and forced her resolve back into battle formation.

Just as she lifted her lids, she saw a pinpoint of light arc through the night and disappear into the water. A moment later, Jackie walked out of the shadows.

"Was that Michael I just missed? The poor darling's been waiting for me." She shrugged her shoulders and slid Tamara a coy smile. "You know how impatient men can be. I'll just go meet him in our..." Her husky laugh echoed around them in the darkness. "...I mean, *his* cabin. Oh, by the way, Tamara." She looked back over her shoulder. "When we dock in Aruba, I'll have a little present for you."

Tamara's common sense screamed she'd need every ounce of strength she possessed to deal with whatever game Jackie was playing. Holding herself very still, she steadily met the glow of Jackie's eyes. "You don't need to give me anything."

Again the husky laugh echoed out into the night, this time sending a shiver down Tamara's bare spine.

"Oh, but I do, darling. I really, really do!"

Day Three—Aruba

The sight of Jackie's perfect red coiffure blowing wildly in the morning breeze drew Tamara irresistibly to the promenade deck railing. She peered over at the dock. What could the actress be up to on the Aruba dock at such an early hour?

She certainly wasn't dressed for exercise class. The skimpy halter top displayed her bosom to perfection and the brief shorts showed off her long shapely legs. Every cabdriver lined up for the disembarking passengers came to rigid attention as she passed by.

Curiosity overruled Tamara's usual indifference to passengers' private affairs. She leaned way over the railing to watch as Jackie spoke to several drivers but kept moving until she reached one in a bright purple T-shirt standing in front of a white Mercedes. She talked animatedly to him for several moments before he leapt into his car and drove away. A premonition, probably induced by Jackie's veiled threat of the night before, caused Tamara to lean forward and memorize the numbers on his license plate.

Maybe she was being neurotic, but there was something about Jackie that provoked her worst suspicions. After the woman disappeared from sight, Tamara turned from the railing to slowly climb the outside stairs of the sun deck. Her confrontation in the moonlight with Shannon on this very deck had given her another restless night. She felt out of focus this morning; off her usual stride. Suddenly, she realized she really hadn't been herself since Shannon had fished her out of the Miami bay.

Taking a deep breath, she quickened her pace. Despite the fact that Michael Shannon was a distraction she couldn't shake, she had a job to do.

The exercise group waiting for her had doubled in size. Obviously, someone had talked, because all the ladies kept glancing through the windows into the next gym. They were destined to be disappointed—Shannon wasn't there this morning. The baggy exercise clothes she'd chosen weren't necessary, after all.

"Good morning, ladies. Everyone have a good evening?"

Shirley and Eileen both laughed and gave her a thumbs-up sign. At least something was going well.

"What's Aruba like, Tamara?" Florence asked, her pale blue eyes crinkling in a smile.

"It's delightfully Dutch. There are even some windmills." Tamara started the group stretching, but instead of turning on the music, she launched into her activities director monologue. "Instead of canals and tulips, you'll find cacti and sand dunes on the shores of a turquoise sea. And there are duty-free shops where you'll meet some of the friendliest people under the Caribbean sun."

"No shopping for me. I'm taking your snorkeling excursion. I'm sure that will be equally appealing."

Tracy winked, obviously recognizing a script when she heard it.

"Sugary beaches and a spectacular underwater paradise," Tamara said, laughing.

"I'm going to try snorkeling, too." Florence looked around sheepishly. "Never too old to try something new."

"Good for you, Florence," Linn said. "Wayne and I are going, and so is Jackie."

"Jackie?"

Some quality Tamara couldn't keep out of her voice caused Tracy to shoot her a sharp look. Recovering quickly, Tamara smiled. "That's great! Do you know if she's coming to exercise this morning? We really should get started with the warm-up."

"Nope. I saw her in the corridor. She said she had some important business to attend to onshore." Linn shrugged good-naturedly. "Jackie probably wants to get a head start on shopping."

Remembering the weight of the suitcases that had almost drowned her, Tamara didn't doubt that in the least. But all through exercise class, a nagging hunch told her that Jackie's business had everything to do with her and the "little present" she'd been promised last night.

She couldn't worry about it, because then Jackie would win for sure. She picked up the pace, deciding to devote all her thoughts to giving the women an excellent workout. For some reason, this morning, she didn't miss a step and didn't mind the perspiration rolling down her back and dampening her hair.

After class, she checked with the purser's office that all the arrangements for the snorkeling trip were completed. Then she quickly showered, dressed in her shore uniform of white blouse and walking shorts and presented herself in the main dining room for breakfast. She liked to go to the passengers, rather than have them try to find her, in case there were any questions about the day's activities.

When she arrived, the room was packed. Since there was open seating, she had to look around for an empty place. Shannon sat across the room, alone, at a table for two. He looked up and waved her over.

For a heartbeat, she hesitated. Her cheek suddenly burned where his lips had brushed so lightly the night before. But she had to meet the ebony challenge glowing in his eyes, so, squaring her shoulders, she moved to join him.

"Good morning, Tamara." He smiled, rose gallantly and pulled out her chair.

Instantly charmed and suspicious at the same time, she glanced at the next table—what the captain referred to as "the Hollywood contingent." "Are you sure you aren't saving this place for Jackie?"

Sheila glanced over and lifted her eyebrows. "Even if we were, she's late as usual, so sit down and enjoy your breakfast."

That authoritative tone brooked no disobedience. Tamara sat, and the rest of the group carried on as if this were business as usual. Inwardly she shivered. She knew the power games played in Hollywood. Right now Sheila had the power, so everyone jumped to her tune.

Tamara drank a sip of orange juice, trying to ignore the fact that Shannon sat beside her, with his leg brushing against hers. The silent apology he smiled at her made her fingers tremble. His dark eyes held depths which drew her, and his smile was pure pleasure to watch. He seemed so pleasant, so normal this morning, so...

Drat the man! She would never be able to swallow any breakfast with him watching her. What was the matter with her, anyway?

It was almost a relief to see Jackie waft into the dining room, attracting everyone's attention. At least Tamara could stop concentrating on Shannon.

Jackie, every hair now perfectly in place, makeup primed for a photo session, surveyed the room carefully. A feeling of dread washed over Tamara.

"There's Jackie!" Tamara jumped to her feet, trying to ward off impending disaster. "I'll let her join you."

"No, no, darling, sit in *my* place for now!" Jackie rushed to the table, gushing with self-importance, and pushed Tamara back down. Her arms were full of newspapers. "It's just perfect that I found you all together. Here's the present I promised you last night."

With a flourish, she thrust two tabloids into Tamara's hands. "Isn't it marvelous? Little Tamara made not one front page, but two!" Her husky laugh drew all the eyes in the room to her. The rest of the passengers seemed mesmerized, waiting to see what would happen next. "I bought every copy on the island so we could distribute them to *everyone.*"

The rest of Jackie's malicious chatter faded in the roar growing in Tamara's ears. There she was, in living color. Twice! In her worst nightmare she couldn't have conjured up a more hideous picture of herself. Her body, with her ruined uniform bunched around her, looked malformed. Her hair appeared colorless and filthy to boot, straggling around her shoulders and over her face. Unfortunately, it didn't cover *all* her face. Her clenched jaw and the blazing anger in her eyes was plain for all the world to see.

In contrast, Jackie looked like a goddess—her white suit spotless, displaying a figure most women would kill for. Her beautiful face managed to convey the message that she was responsible for the rescue.

Standing between them, Michael Shannon looked magnificent. Even drenched, his clinging suit showed off the physique millions of soap fans drooled over daily. His wet hair hugged the chiseled features the camera loved.

Beauties and the beast.

It couldn't have been more apparent. The headlines should have proclaimed Two Of The World's Beautiful People Take Pity On A Poor Bedraggled Creature.

Inside the paper, the picture of the gorgeous soap star kissing the creature from the sea was even more humiliating.

Tamara's stomach clenched with anger. Finally, she looked up from the hideous picture. Jackie's self-satisfied smile told her the whole story. A totally uncharitable, totally irrational, but totally justifiable urge to wipe that smile off her face took root in Tamara's heart.

"I know, darling, you're speechless with delight." Her eyes wide in feigned innocence, Jackie scattered papers over the other tables so all could see. "Look, they even spelled Tamara's name correctly. I speak from experience, darling. *That* does not always happen."

Everyone looked at Tamara, silently waiting for her reaction. Not by a flicker would she let them see how this wounded her pride. She didn't need their approval and she certainly didn't want their pity!

Any thought that Shannon might leap to her defense was scotched by the look on his face. Completely blank, it showed no emotion that she could read. He simply looked through her, as if none of this made a bit of difference.

Spurred on by the power of her anger, Tamara slowly smiled and tucked both papers under her arm. "Jackie, what fun this will be to save in my scrapbook. I can't thank you enough! What can I ever do to repay you?"

"Oh, darling, how sweet." Jackie patted her in a gesture of mock friendship. "You don't need to repay me, really you don't."

"Oh, but I do. I really, really do." Tamara repeated Jackie's words of the previous night as she backed away from the table.

She turned and walked slowly out of the dining room, whispers following in her wake. In the corridor she came face-to-face with John, the purser. The traitor! He actually tried to hide a paper behind his back.

"If you say one word, I'll strangle you!" she said hotly.

"Can I tell you I'm your assistant for the snorkeling excursion today?" he offered timidly.

"Fine! Meet me at the minibuses at nine-thirty sharp!"

It was a mark of her rage that he didn't give her a hard time with his usual wry sense of humor. After all, on board, he outranked her by a mile.

That made her pause. Really, the pictures were kind of funny. If it had been anyone but Jackie...if *he* hadn't been there to witness her reaction...she probably would have seen it in perspective and laughed right along with the others. But Jackie had deliberately, with malice aforethought, tried to humiliate her in front of the entire ship.

She knew it, and everyone else knew it. The best revenge would be to carry on as if nothing had happened. But somewhere, somehow, she would repay the favor!

By excursion time, she was in command of herself again. She assigned John to the minibus carrying the soap opera cast. At least she'd have a few minutes of peace on the way to the snorkeling cove.

Just as the driver was closing the door of her van, a large tanned hand curled around the frame. The door slid open and Shannon stepped in, dressed in black trunks and a neon yellow and black T-shirt.

"What are you doing here?" she snapped, then softened her tone to conceal the strain in her voice. "You're supposed to be on the other bus."

"There's no room," he lied. "You'll have to take me."

"Fine. There's a seat at the back of the bus. It's not very comfortable, though," she muttered, darting a parting glance at him. She heard Joe and Irma gasp in surprise from the seat behind her.

"It will be perfect," he said smoothly.

His reply echoed in her ears as they bumped along the dirt road to the cove. This ride was enough to jar Rip van Winkle awake, especially back where Michael sprawled, his legs stretched out before him as if he were perfectly at ease.

He alighted from the bus looking completely happy. Wretch, Tamara thought as she began organizing the participants into groups of novice or experienced snorkelers.

The inexperienced group was smaller and she happily assigned them to John. She justified her decision by explaining he would be the better teacher. Of course, that choice also saddled him with most of the *Another Hospital* cast.

Jackie, wearing the skimpiest bikini decency allowed, opted to stay on the beach and watch. She demanded that Harry remain with her when no one else volunteered.

Shannon hung back until she identified the group Tamara would be leading, then claimed to be experienced. He listened intently as she issued instructions, peering at her through slightly narrowed eyes, as if he were weighing *her* ability.

"Stay clear of the coral reef. The tide out there can get pretty fierce, and, just when you least expect it, will push you onto the coral. So please, stay to the left where there is plenty to see. Or, if you prefer, follow me."

She turned to get her equipment, including a small knife which she strapped to her thigh. Shannon's intent stare made her extremely self-conscious while alerting her that she would have to keep an eye out for him just in case he wasn't as experienced as he claimed. Everyone else was putting on his or her gear or helping one another with the life vests, but he just stood in front of her, waiting.

Finally exasperated past patience, she spread her legs, dug her toes deeply into the warm sand, placed her hands on her hips, tilted her head back and glared up at him.

"What are you doing?" she demanded.

The sun shot glints of light off his shiny hair and played along the high cheekbones above his sweetly curled mouth. "I'm just watching out for you. Everyone should have a buddy when they snorkel."

A tightness curled in her chest. "I thought chivalry was dead," she quipped after finding her voice.

"No, it's only wounded." He laughed. "I know Jackie's on the warpath. She can't help herself. She's been Alexandria for so long, she can't help playing the vixen in real life. It happens to actors sometimes. I'm just here to run interference for you."

"Where were you this morning when I needed you?" She could have bitten her tongue off for betraying her hurt pride.

"If I'd intervened, it would have made things worse."

"Why? It isn't your fault she's such a witch." She lowered her voice diplomatically, feeling oddly comforted by his words.

"In a way, it is." He leaned toward her, moving so quickly she couldn't retreat without tripping, since her feet had burrowed into the sand. She had no choice but to stay put as his body shadowed the sun and his clean male scent surrounded her.

"She's acting this way because she knows I want you. And I've wanted you since that kiss now immortalized in every scandal sheet on the globe. The next time I kiss you, Tamara, I promise there won't be an audience."

His blunt words struck her like a blow. She swayed and he caught her by her shoulders, leaving his hands there even when she was steady again. They burned into her flesh as she studied his face. Even this close, in revealing sunlight, he was too handsome for his own good.

Too handsome for *her* good.

Still reeling from the morning's emotions, she lost her temper. "Shannon, or should I just call you Mr. Diamond? That speech sounds like something straight out of your show. Perhaps you have the same affliction as Jackie. Can you tell the difference between real life and tape? Just who is it that wants me—Stephen Diamond or Michael Shannon? Or is there any difference?"

That barb hit home. She was free instantly. He stepped back two paces to stare at her, his eyes filling with confusion. "Would you believe me if I told you I'm not sure anymore?"

His honesty was surprising and more than she wanted to deal with at the moment. "Confusion, I believe." Her laughter came out in little gasps of self-preservation. "But if you want to watch over me, you're going to have to get wet. I'm going snorkeling."

THE WATER SOOTHED Michael when he plunged into the ocean after her. He hadn't meant to be so blunt.

Last night, he'd realized he needed to slow down. There was something about this woman that made him want to protect her, from Jackie and the press, and maybe even from himself.

After witnessing how she'd handled the situation with Jackie that morning, something had subtly shifted in his highly anticipated seduction of Miss Tamara Hayes. He admired her. Few women could hold their own with Jackie—none when she was on the warpath, he'd have bet before this day. Yet Tamara had more than managed.

He'd seen the tiny flicker of surprise in Jackie's eyes when Tamara kept her cool, even got some of her own back with that last thinly veiled threat. He hadn't missed that, and neither had Jackie. Sooner or later, there would be hell to pay between the two and he wanted to be around to see it.

For now, he would just enjoy the view. A few yards ahead, Tamara's body, encased in a neon orange tank suit, shimmered with the light filtering through the water. The contour of her breasts shifted seductively beneath the thin material as she stroked smoothly through the water, stopping to point out anything of interest to the few swimmers around her.

For a moment, the memory of those breasts filling his hands at their first meeting disconcerted him. Then he kicked forward, getting ahead of the group, but never too far from her.

She motioned to a school of bright-colored striped fish and swam toward them, away from the group and him. He gave chase and she swam faster, leaving the group behind. He deliberately brushed against her, thigh to thigh, just to get her attention. The contact held a languishing sensuality as the waves tangled their bodies delicately before pulling them apart.

Someday he'd make love to her in the water. It would be poetically fitting considering how they'd met.

A distant noise disturbed the tranquillity. Suddenly, Tamara surfaced. He stayed beside her, tearing off his mask when he heard a commotion. Side by side they trod water, their fins easily keeping them afloat while they looked to see what was going on.

Finally, he saw Irma standing on the shore screaming at the top of her lungs while gesturing wildly out to sea.

Tamara gasped. "It's Joe! He's gotten too close to the reef."

His hand curled around her arm before she could move. "I'll go. He outweighs you by almost a hundred pounds. If he needs help, I'm better equipped. You go calm Irma. And call the rescue squad."

Her green eyes looked huge framed by wet spiky lashes, but she kept her cool. "He's my responsibility, but you're right. Be careful of the current."

Ridiculous as it was, damned if he didn't feel chivalrous! She must trust him to let him do this for her.

His powerful crawl got him out to the reef in no time. True to character, Joe was so absorbed in snapping underwater pictures, he had no idea he'd swum out so far until Michael pointed to the danger. Apologizing all the way, he allowed Michael to haul him back to shore.

Between an enthusiastic hug from Irma and Joe's hardy handshake, he found himself searching the beach for Tamara.

"Oh, darling, you were magnificent, as always!" Jackie gushed, careful not to get too close. She wouldn't want to get her expensive bathing ensemble wet.

Anything and everything she did had stopped surprising him five years ago. He had tried, over and over, to discourage her, but nothing worked. Right now she wore a sheer white cover-up and a large hat to shade her face, yet somehow managed to broadcast sexuality. She just couldn't get it through her head that her efforts left him cold.

"Thanks, Jackie. See you later." He brushed past her to move down the beach toward Tamara.

Everyone was out of the water, happy after the excitement, to relax on the extra-large beach towels supplied by the ship. Michael snatched the last towel out of the purser's hands, spread it over the hot sand and threw himself down.

Sooner or later, Tamara was going to have to come over and say something about Joe. He rested his head on his arm and studied her as she settled the group, offering cool drinks and sunscreen. Nothing seemed to faze her; no near catastrophe, no petty spite. She just did her job, making everyone else comfortable.

Then she turned and looked at him. The fierce Caribbean sun had already turned her fair skin pink.

Resisting the urge to motion her over, he waited until her shadow fell across his body. Then he patted the blanket beside him. "Sit down. You're getting burned. Let me put some lotion on your back and shoulders."

"Michael, I owe you." Sighing, she dropped beside him. "Thank you. You saved Joe's life."

His gaze lingered on her wide green eyes, and damn if he didn't feel that knight-of-the-round-table feeling again. It wasn't a role he often played, offscreen.

He pushed a finger against her upper arm to show the color she was getting. "If you want to thank me, let me put some sunscreen on you. How are we going to dance tonight if you're burned?"

She sucked in a deep breath that lifted her breasts beneath the quickly drying swimsuit and flung herself facedown on the towel.

"You owe me, remember?" he teased, moving toward her.

Laughing, she twisted her hair in a knot. "Okay. Just behave yourself in case anyone's watching."

He took a quick look around. No one appeared to be looking their way. For the first time in a long time, Michael felt like any other guy. No one was snapping pictures or asking for autographs.

He could just be anonymous here on the beach—a guy with his girl. Her muscles were firm and strong beneath his palms. Perhaps she was a little tense. All he knew was that running his hands up her long slender legs made him *a lot* tense.

She sighed as he smoothed the lotion over the small of her back. She looked so beautiful stretched out with the sun golden on her skin. She lifted an arm demandingly and his hands stroked it eagerly. He wanted to turn her over and strip the tank suit right off her. He wanted to bury his face in her breasts, taste her sweetness, make her totally his.

Stop it, you ass, he commanded himself. He'd promised the next time he kissed her, there would be no witnesses. It might be torture to continue rubbing her body with lotion, but he did it to prove to himself he could behave if he had to.

"How'd you get to be an activities director?" he asked, forcing himself to sound normal.

She turned her face toward him without opening her eyes. "I like people and I needed a job. How'd you become an actor?"

"By accident. I went out to L.A. to become a director. Somewhere along the line, I lost sight of that dream."

Acutely aware of any small movement she made, Michael felt her grow still beneath his palms. A moment later, a shudder vibrated along her warm pliant skin.

Before he could ask what was wrong, Wayne ran up, kicking sand on the blanket, breaking the mood.

"Hey, Mike, Jackie's down the beach at the bar. I think she's sick, or something."

Tamara struggled to sit, automatically adjusting her straps. Michael reluctantly pulled her to her feet. Just when things were going so well. Leave it to Jackie.

"Would you like me to call for the ship's doctor?" she asked, throwing a worried look down the beach.

"No, let me handle it," Shannon said. This would be a good time to tell Jackie to lay off Tamara. "Wait here. I'll take care of this and be right back."

He followed Wayne toward a chickee bar about a half mile away. As they got closer, the sound of steel drums echoed toward them. The bar's thatched roof shaded about a dozen tables right at the ocean's edge.

It felt much cooler under the roof, but Jackie sagged in her chair. Linn was patting her hand and fanning her at the same time. When Linn looked up and saw him, her eyes were glassy with tears. What the hell was going on?

Quickly she bent her head, scrubbing her wet cheeks with her fists like a child before whispering something to Jackie.

He was halfway across the room when Jackie lifted her head and looked at him. She *was* pale, but what convinced him of her distress was her total lack of come-on to the multitude of males around her. If this was an act, it was one of her better ones.

"Thank you for coming, darling. It's this dreadful sun. I'm afraid it's given me a headache." She flashed him a weak smile. "I really think I should go back to the ship and rest. Michael, darling, would you mind terribly getting me a taxi? There must be at least one around here somewhere."

"Believe it or not, there are two." He motioned to the short man lounging against a black Saab.

"Not him!" Jackie shrieked, rising to her feet with remarkable strength. "I want the other one!" She gestured toward the driver with the door already open to a white Mercedes.

"Why him?" He was beginning to smell a rat.

"Because his cab looks safer. Besides, a Mercedes is always better sprung. If I have to endure another bumpy ride like the one we had out here, my head will split open!"

He believed her. That ride had been a killer. And he suspected Tamara had enjoyed every jolt he'd had to endure.

He led Jackie, who was clinging to him for support, to the open cab.

"Sir, could you please take me back to the *Diamond Queen* over as smooth a route as possible?" Jackie cooed.

"Sure, lady, I know just the way."

Suddenly, Michael felt strong arms propel him forward and before he could react, he found himself sitting next to Jackie on the back seat. The door slammed and the cab took off like a bat out of hell.

Damn! And what would Tamara make of this?

"This is just like old times, isn't it, darling?" Sighing, Jackie pressed her breast against his forearm. "I've never gotten over you, Michael. I don't think I ever will." Her hand settled on his lap with such subtle grace, he took a moment to admire her technique before he removed it. Placing it back on her own lap, he patted her fingers.

"Good try, Jackie. But if memory serves, you've been engaged six times since we broke it off. You've lived with at least one other guy and came within hours of eloping to Vegas with George. Remember George, Jackie?" he teased. "The man you declared—to everyone, including every newspaper reporter in the free world—was the love of your life. The man you wanted to live in a rose-covered cottage and have a dozen children with."

She blinked up at him, sadness washing a shadow through her magnificent violet eyes. "I almost made a dreadful mistake, but something cried out for me to stop before it was too late. I can only think it was my true feelings for you that were refusing to be denied."

His bark of laughter was drowned out by the grinding of brakes as the car came to a halt.

Smiling, the driver turned to them. "Here, delicious island drinks served."

"Oh, darling, look! It's a real windmill! Please, Michael," she said as she tugged playfully on his arm. "A drink might help my headache. I didn't have one on the beach."

He'd definitely been set up. But now was as good a time as any to set Jackie straight. Then he'd go right back to the beach and Tamara.

The driver already had Jackie's door open and she was sliding out eagerly. If he catered to her whim, maybe he could use her good mood to get her to agree to back off from Tamara.

"Just one quick drink, Jackie," he warned, stepping out of the cab. "We have to be back by five and the ship sails at six. And I have a few things I want to make clear to you."

"Of course, darling," she said, laughing, already gliding through the picturesque entryway.

The windmill had been converted into a small restaurant. Inside was cool and dim and empty. They settled into a corner table overlooking a tangle of greenery that had an exotic scent that reminded him of Tamara.

"Isn't this delightful, darling?" Jackie glanced eagerly around. "How romantic, Michael. We have the place all to ourselves."

Two large strawberry-colored drinks adorned with paper umbrellas were placed in front of them. "Specialty of the house," the owner said, nodding.

"Thank you." Michael glanced at his watch. "Will you tell our driver we'll be ready to go in ten minutes?"

"Sorry. He say he have errand. Will be right back."

"Then call us another taxi."

"No phone. No worry. He be back."

"Of course, he will." Jackie curled her fingers over his on the white tablecloth. "Michael, darling, relax. We won't miss the boat."

"WE HAVE to be back on board by five," John warned. "Is everyone accounted for?"

Tamara had known for the last half hour exactly who was missing. Her chivalrous knight had obviously defected to the enemy, a fact that caused her some painful and definitely unwelcome pangs of disappointment.

Not that she'd actually believed that line of his about coming right back! Well, maybe she had believed him just a little bit, she admitted grudgingly. That only doubled her disillusionment.

"I'm missing four," she declared firmly, taking herself in hand. "Wait here and I'll go look for them down the beach."

She slipped espadrilles on her feet, picked up her beach bag and started off along the sand. Florence and Tracy, who had spent the day learning to snorkel together, waved at her.

"Can we help?" Tracy shouted.

"I'll be right back!" she called out, making her way slowly down the beach. Although the hot sun warmed her back through her cover-up, she wouldn't suffer any sunburn tonight. Shannon had seen to that with his clever hands rhythmically stroking her, wiping away all her good sense.

The beat of the steel drums matched the headache throbbing behind her eyes by the time she reached the chickee bar. Wayne and Linn were just starting off in her direction; they seemed surprised to see her. She glanced beyond them expectantly.

"Aren't Michael and Jackie here with you?" she asked.

"They were. But Jackie had such a bad headache, she wanted to go back to the ship."

"And Mike." Linn giggled nervously, interrupting him. "Uh, Mike, was…kind of shanghaied. Some guy pushed him into the cab with her."

Warning bells went off in her head. "Wayne, what kind of a cab was it?"

"Jackie fussed, as usual, and insisted on a Mercedes," he said.

"A white Mercedes, no doubt, with a driver wearing a purple T-shirt." Tamara sighed.

"Jeez, how did you know that?" Linn asked.

"Just a lucky guess. Would you mind waiting here while I call and make sure they're on board?"

It was several minutes before she reached the ship, and another fifteen before it was confirmed that neither Michael nor Jackie had reboarded.

She was more than disappointed now. She was mad! And she wasn't sure whom she was madder at—Jackie for pulling this stunt, or Michael for being so gullible. She slowly replaced the receiver, trying to decide how she could thwart Jackie's little game.

After recruiting Wayne to explain the situation to the purser and sending the young couple down the beach, she walked over to a driver half-asleep in his taxi. Reaching into her bag, she pulled out the roll of twenty-dollar bills she always carried ashore for emergencies. Peeling off two, she waved them in front of him.

"There's two more of these if you find the driver who was here earlier, the one wearing a purple T-shirt and driving the white Mercedes."

A toothy grin split his narrow sun-weathered face. "Get in."

They found the Mercedes at their third stop. The car was last in line at one of the big resort hotels that dotted the island. She couldn't understand one word of the conversation her driver shouted out his window to the man in the purple T-shirt, but whatever was said prompted her driver to open the car door, usher her out of his cab and into the other one.

"Lady, happy?" He grinned.

"Yes. Very." Nodding, she folded more bills into his palm.

Twisting around in the driver's seat, her new chauffeur gave her a once-over through narrowed eyes. "Looking for me?"

"Whatever the beautiful lady paid you this morning, I'll double it if you take me where she is," she said.

He whistled through his teeth. "Much money, lady. You sure?"

"Very sure. And there's another twenty if you get me there quickly."

She almost regretted the bribe as she bounced from one side of the cab to the other. The Mercedes roared down narrow lanes and took curves at breakneck speed before it shrieked to a halt in front of a windmill restaurant. Just like the pictures in the guidebooks, she thought. *Couldn't you do any better than this, Jackie?*

He gestured with his head. "Inside."

"Don't leave!" she commanded.

"No worry. Lady no pay me yet."

Inside, from the vestibule, she could hear their voices arguing.

"I mean it, Jackie! I'd better not find out you planned this. Damn, it's straight out of the script! We've been stranded on an island together twice in the last three years!"

"Darling, of course I wouldn't plan such a thing!" Jackie cried with just the faintest thread of hurt feelings in her voice. "We won't miss the silly boat. I'm sure the driver will be back in time."

Revenge, sweet revenge! Tamara felt positively giddy. Smiling, she stepped over the threshold.

"Surprise! Your driver's back!" she called out sweetly. "And look who he's brought with him."

Jackie's shocked expression vanished, replaced by a loathing that turned her face into an ugly mask. Abruptly, she became all wide-eyed wonder. If Tamara hadn't watched the transformation herself, she wouldn't have believed it possible, but there Jackie stood, startled pleasure masking her true feelings.

"Look, Michael! I told you we'd be rescued. And by our very own Tamara."

Tamara finally had to glance at Michael. Even with an angry flush coloring his skin and the nerve throbbing along his jawline, to her, he looked dazzling. How had this happened? The man was an *actor,* for goodness' sake! And incredibly gullible, she reminded herself.

"If we leave right now, there is a slim chance we won't miss the ship." She turned away pointedly, as much to free herself from the allure of his face as to hurry them along.

"Let's go." He threw money on the table and stalked out the door. Could he be upset with her for having caught them together? she wondered.

Jackie didn't seem to mind a bit, at least after that first unguarded look. The actress strolled after him as if she had all the time in the world. It was all Tamara could do not to push her sashaying rear end into the taxi.

At least the driver still had the engine running.

"Want to get there quick, mon?" he asked when Tamara slipped into the front seat beside him.

She gripped the seat edge with iron fingers before nodding.

They sped at a breakneck pace along the twisting dirt back roads, careening around corners and leaving a trail of dust behind them. When the cab reached a congested ribbon of asphalt, the driver gunned the engine and, with no apparent thought of safety, cut in and out of traffic like a madman.

The precarious ride silenced Jackie's inane chatter, but each and every jolting moment, she could feel Shannon's eyes boring into the back of her head. Was he angry? Embarrassed? Relieved? She didn't dare turn to look at him and she couldn't bear to ask. He maintained a stoic silence the whole trip.

The driver pulled up to the dock, stopping only inches from the water with a fishtail that would have made Al Unser nervous. In the distance, the *Dia-*

mond Queen steamed majestically out of the harbor, blowing her horn in farewell.

"Damn!" Shannon finally broke his silence.

His low mutter caused Jackie's lush mouth to curl into a pout as she batted her eyelashes at him and smiled helplessly.

Disgusted, Tamara paid off the cabbie and ushered her two charges toward the harbor master's office. "Don't worry, Mr. Shannon, I've taken care of it."

The harbormaster had a pilot boat waiting for them. As they boarded, she gave a silent thanks to S&B's legendary efficiency. They were not the first to miss an embarkation, even if they were the first to do so on purpose. At least the ship wasn't so far away that they had to stay here overnight and catch a flight to the next port of call.

Tamara kept a tight grip on her facade of professionalism, but she didn't attempt to be cordial; she was too mad for that. She turned her back on her charges and spoke quietly to the pilot as he radioed ahead.

By the time they arrived at the *Diamond Queen*, the steel supply door was open and ready. A sailor tossed a grappling hook down and pulled the smaller boat alongside. Almost, but not quite, Tamara felt a twinge of sympathy for Jackie as a rope ladder snaked toward them.

"Is this *really* necessary?" the actress asked coldly.

If a look could kill, Tamara would surely be dead. "I'm afraid so. It's really quite simple," she replied with a smile. "Don't worry, I'll be right behind you."

Jackie looked up and saw the throng of enthralled passengers lining the railing at the same time Tamara did. Immediately, her body posture altered. She flung back her head until her flaming curls cascaded down her bare back and blew kisses to the crowd.

"Just do it, Jackie," Shannon ordered, holding the ladder steady.

Any concern vanished from Tamara's mind. Jackie played her graceful ascent like a pro.

"You go next," Michael said.

She couldn't misinterpret the message in his stare. Grateful for her remaining anger, she denied his order quite easily. "As ship's representative, I go last. It's protocol."

"Go now. If you fall, I'll catch you."

"I never fall, Mr. Shannon."

"We're regressing. The name's Michael, remember? And there's always a first time, Tamara." As if to verify his words, the sea rolled and a chasm opened between the boats.

A shadow cast by the looming ship turned his eyes chocolate and his smile melting. It just wasn't fair.

The pilot stood behind him blatantly listening to every word, a vapid smile covering his face. One hundred passengers hung over the railing, watching. She looked up to see Jackie lifted aboard by two burly crewmen. Once again, Joe Wright risked life and limb trying to record the moment for posterity. He actually hung over the railing by one hand while pointing the video camera with the other. She would definitely have to speak to him about taking such risks.

Mumbling to herself, she gripped the rope ladder in firm fingers and climbed. She could feel Shannon right behind her. Every inch of her skin burned in nervous embarrassment. Her dancer's instinct seemed to have deserted her entirely and she fumbled clumsily at each rung.

Then her foot slipped off the rope entirely. Panic shot through her. Instantly, she felt Shannon's body cover hers protectively, his arm muscles bulging as he held them both steady while she regained her footing.

She could feel her cheeks blaze. Why was this man always rescuing her?

And after Jackie had climbed up so daintily. It just wasn't fair!

At least he didn't further embarrass her with an "I told you so."

His hand splayed across her backside, urging her upward. That was all the motivation she needed to scurry up the remaining rungs into the waiting arms of the crewmen.

A crowd surged around Shannon, giving her the chance to escape. She was *not* running away, she was simply doing her duty and promptly reporting the incident to her superior, she told herself.

Twenty minutes later, she'd entered the last of her report into her computer. When the office door slowly opened, she tensed every muscle in defense, expecting Shannon. It would be just like him to follow her.

"Jackie!" Her defiance quickly shifted to dismay.

Still dressed in the flimsy excuse for a bathing suit cover-up, Jackie clicked the door shut and pressed herself against it. "Darling! We really must have a little chat. I've been very naughty but then, so have you. Now, shall we call it a draw and become friends?"

Not for one instant did Tamara buy the brilliant smile or the charming voice. But she had a job to do and she couldn't do it if she had to worry about Jackie sneaking up on her every second. A truce it would be, but an uneasy one at best. Instinct made her stand so Jackie wouldn't loom so tall over her.

"We aren't in competition. I'm sorry we somehow got off on the wrong foot."

"Oh, but darling, I'm afraid we are in a bit of a competition. Of course, I don't blame you." Jackie shrugged her beautiful shoulders. "Michael is positively impossible to resist throwing oneself at. But you will try, won't you, darling?"

She clenched her jaw but was unable to bite back the angry retort that roared up into her throat. "I think perhaps it's the other way around."

"Oh my, our little Tamara has a temper." Jackie's silvery laughter filled the cabin, giving her goose bumps. "I knew you were just too deliciously sweet to be believed. I can hardly wait to uncover all your other secrets."

She slipped out the door before Tamara had a chance to answer. As a threat, Jackie's words were mild. She hid no secrets. But knowing Jackie's flair for the dramatic, she would have to remain on her guard.

She sank into her chair and sighed deeply. How could she ever have thought having soap stars on board would be fun?

She'd actually believed she had put the past firmly behind her so she could deal with these actors in a purely professional manner. And, except for Shannon and Jackie, she was doing her job just fine.

At least it seemed as if everyone *else* was having a great time. And it was her job to see that it all continued.

She couldn't dare admit, even to herself, that Jackie had spoken the truth for once. Michael Shannon was impossible for her to resist.

Day Four—At Sea

The next morning, Tamara found Joe up on the sun deck, Irma hovering at his side, offering the most impractical suggestions as he recorded Shannon entertaining a group of passengers with funny stories about backstage at *Another Hospital*. He was wearing the tight black bathing suit and a black knit shirt that showcased his virility.

Sometimes, he appeared quite sincere, especially when it came to his fans. She wanted to trust him, to believe he was as genuine as he seemed; but after her experiences in LaLa Land, it was hard to trust anyone in show business. Even someone who only yesterday had been a real hero.

She put on her happiest smile and stepped in front of the video camera, waving brightly for posterity's sake.

Irma blinked at her in surprise. "Put the camera down, Joe. I think Tamara wants to talk to us."

Dutifully, he obeyed. But she could see he kept his finger hovering over the power button just in case another video opportunity presented itself.

"I understand your eagerness to record these events for your friends back home, but I must caution you against taking unnecessary risks."

"Risks? I wouldn't do that!" Joe protested, bewilderment widening his watery green eyes.

"I guess I just got a little concerned when I saw you hanging over the railing yesterday."

"But I got a great shot of Michael savin' you when you slipped. Want to see it?"

Before she could protest, he had pushed the proper switches on the camera and was reviewing his latest effort. After a moment, he exclaimed, "Here it is. Just look through the viewer, right here, Tamara."

She watched Jackie's graceful progress up the rope ladder, then her own reluctant start and finally her slip as the rope ladder swayed against the side of the ship. She sucked in an involuntary breath. She looked so helpless and confused, which she'd vowed never to be again. When the video showed Shannon absorbing the weight of her body until she regained her footing, she stopped breathing or thinking and felt his touch again.

"Aren't they great pictures, Tamara?" Joe was completely sincere, certain he'd captured a great moment on film.

But the curl of desire on her mouth, the way her eyelids narrowed in pleasure as Shannon cupped her to his body didn't come across as a great moment to Tamara. It was a distinct and unpleasant shock. She pushed the camera into Joe's hands as if to deny the evidence of her own eyes.

"What's so interesting?" Shannon's question startled her. When had he come up to stand beside her?

"I'm showin' Tamara my footage from yesterday when you two were comin' back on board. Here, take a look."

Rigid with embarrassment, she stood helplessly by as he lifted the video camera to his eye. Any faint hope that he might not notice the purely involuntary response of her body to his fled the instant he turned from the camera to look at her. Gold from the sun seemed to reflect from the depths of his eyes.

"Very interesting, Joe. Thanks for sharing it with me." His words might be for the Wrights, but his penetrating stare never left her face. "Tamara and I will see you both, later."

His hand closed around her arm as he propelled her toward the outside deck. She told herself she allowed him this liberty only to avoid an unpleasant scene.

"What's all this? Where are we going?" she hissed under the guise of a tight smile.

"Somewhere private where we can talk about yesterday. My cabin."

"I think not!" She broke away. "I'm on duty," she declared, throwing out the only excuse that came to her.

"I read the daily schedule and there's no fan event tonight." He folded his arms across his chest and smiled at her. "So, logically, you must have the evening off."

She thought of lying to him, then dismissed the idea as too cowardly. "As a matter of fact, I do have the evening off." At the look of triumph on his face, she continued smoothly, "However, I have plans." The half lie didn't cause her even a twinge of guilt.

"Would you consider changing them and having dinner with me in my cabin?"

She knew what she should say, was even forming her refusal in her head, when her mouth opened and betrayed her. "Would seven o'clock be convenient for you?"

"Perfect," he answered softly.

She fled then, away from his hot gaze and satisfied smile. What was happening to her? Well, she might have foolishly agreed to meet him for dinner, but it certainly wouldn't be the evening he obviously envisioned! She'd make certain of that.

MICHAEL PACED his small cabin, glancing at his watch every few minutes. Tamara was late.

He paused, poured himself a glass of champagne from the bottle chilling in a silver cooler and glanced around the room. The low dining cart, lavishly set for two, took up most of the free space, making the bed assume a predominant threat.

He frowned. Tamara might not believe it, and he could hardly accept it himself, but he hadn't meant to set the scene for seduction. He wanted, needed to get the record straight about yesterday afternoon. For some reason, having her approval really mattered to him.

He'd been struck by what he'd seen captured on Joe Wright's videotape; something inside him longed to explore that unguarded expression on Tamara's face. She wasn't as indifferent to him as she'd like him to believe.

But Tamara was fighting her feelings, and no matter what, he knew she would never just use him as other women had. She was too genuine for that. Funny, how he'd sensed that from the very first day.

Anticipation roiled in his gut. He threw himself onto the love seat and took another long drink of icy champagne.

A soft knock raised his spirits. He uncurled slowly; maybe seduction wasn't so far from his mind, after all.

Jackie posed outside his door, a temperamental pout on her bright red lips. It was like being doused by a cold shower.

"Why, darling, you were expecting me!" She brushed past him into the room. "You remembered how I love eating in bed after making love."

Once her throaty laugh would have excited him, but now it merely irritated. "What are you doing here, Jackie?"

He slammed the door and stopped her from flinging herself across the bed. "What are you up to, Jackie? You can see I'm expecting someone."

Batting her lashes, she leaned heavily into him. "You could always change your plans, darling. I'll make it worth your while."

None too gently he gripped her soft shoulders and pushed her back toward the door. "Good try. *Good night,* Jackie."

"Michael, stop!" Twisting around, she pressed herself against his chest once again. "You can't really be serious about pursuing that little nobody. She's probably got a secret yen to be an actress and thinks you can help her. Don't they all? Really, darling, you're so gullible." She sighed, deep and forlorn, as if she were really concerned about him.

"It's not a good idea for *you* to dredge up that particular accusation."

"Darling! How can you still believe I was using our relationship to enhance my own career!"

Magically, tears appeared on her thick lashes. God! Maybe she did deserve her two Emmy nominations.

"Michael, darling, I—"

Interrupted by a definite knock, she swung away, and before he could stop her, pulled the door open.

Tamara, dressed in her camouflaging white uniform, blinked in surprise, then smiled sweetly. "Good evening, Jackie. Will you be joining us?"

Michael was surprised at her composure. But then, so was Jackie.

She missed a beat, then tossed her hair over her shoulder playfully. "Silly, darling, I always allow Michael his little games." She blew him a kiss. "Let me know when you're done with her, Michael darling."

The deliberate insult caused a flush to spread over Tamara's face. He grabbed her hand before she could bolt and pulled her into his room. Her eyes touched on the table set for two, then settled on the bed. She flinched and immediately he set her free. He was afraid to say anything that might upset her even more. Slowly, she moved to the silver plate covers and lifted them.

"Chateaubriand for two." She gazed at him out of clear eyes. "I suppose there's extra béarnaise, and *tiramisu* for dessert. Who did you bribe?"

Beauty and brains. He liked that. In fact, he admitted, he hadn't found anything about Tamara he didn't like.

"I didn't have to bribe anyone. I told my steward-ess I wanted dinner for two in my cabin. When I told her you were my guest, she volunteered the informa-tion. I gather everyone on staff marvels that you can eat like this and still keep your figure."

"I have great metabolism."

Chuckling, he slid his eyes over the concealing blouse and skirt. "You certainly do."

She glared at him. "This is ridiculous! You might be gullible enough to fall for Jackie's ploy yesterday, but please don't imagine I'm stupid enough to be taken in by this setup!" She flung back her head and tendrils of moonbeam hair fell around her face, escaping from the tight bun she wore. "I came here to talk to you in my professional capacity. I should have known bet-ter."

"You did know better. But you came, anyway." Shifting his body, he blocked her escape. "I have one thing to say before you disappear. I'm many things, but gullible isn't one of them. L.A. eats gullible fools for lunch and spits out their remains by dinner."

Tamara hadn't looked this frightened half-drowned or clinging to that rope ladder. Unable to resist, he cupped her face with gentle fingers. "Don't be fright-ened of me, Tamara," he whispered, searching her stricken eyes for answers.

"Why are you doing this?"

Her tears were real. They tasted salty on his lips as he kissed them from her cheeks. "You know why," he whispered against her mouth. He tangled his fingers in the heavy weight of her hair, setting it free to fall around her face. Its fragrant silkiness tickled him as he nuzzled her throat hungrily.

She stood like a statue under his tender assault. After a moment, she gasped softly, "I didn't come here for this."

Excitement spiraled through him as he pulled her into his embrace, until he could feel every soft curve and hollow of her body.

"Yes, you did." Slanting his mouth over her parted lips, he stopped her protests once and for all.

She hadn't come here for this! Her mind protested even as her body betrayed her; just as it had done on the dance floor, just as it had done yesterday. For some inexplicable reason, her body fit into his, like the old silver spoons in her grandmother's drawer. Somehow, he broke down all her barriers.

"Why are you afraid?" he whispered so gently against her quivering lips, she thought she might have imagined his words.

She said nothing, rendered speechless by the deafening panicked heartbeat in her ears. His smile was so genuine, sweet enough that she could feast on its honey.

Tamara understood physical desire. She'd experienced it once or twice; but this was entirely different. She could feel herself sipping out of control. Frightened as she'd never been in all her life, she whimpered deep in her throat. His hands ceased their gentle exploration of her waist and hips to stroke her shoulders reassuringly.

That one act of kindness stirred such an overwhelming response, she swayed into him. The low light in the room outlined the beauty of his face, yet even here, held in his arms, she couldn't read his eyes.

"You really are afraid, aren't you?" he said.

She allowed him to enfold her in his arms, allowed him to draw her down beside him on the love seat. With a tenderness that stopped her breathing, he placed her head on his shoulder.

"Don't worry, Tamara. All I want to do tonight is talk."

"About what?" The words came out in a little croak, forced through her tight throat. She couldn't decide if she was relieved or disappointed.

"About you. Me." He stroked her loosened hair. "I'm really not a very frightening person, you know. Don't believe everything you read in those rags. I graduated from Northwestern University in theater arts, then went to L.A. to become a director. I never planned to become an actor, it just happened. The business is like that."

She knew exactly how the business worked; she had vowed to put it forever behind her. She had also promised herself not to be sucked in like Ally had been.

Yet here she was, literally lying in the arms of temptation.

Had she wanted to tear herself away from him in self-defense, she knew she no longer had the strength of purpose. Her cheek rested against his chest, and through the thin fabric of his shirt, she could feel his warmth and smell the tangy scent of his soap. His hands weren't holding her prisoner, they simply stroked her softly, soothingly. It seemed rude, even foolish, to disturb them.

From across the room, a gentle knock sounded. She knew she should be relieved to be saved from her own foolishness, but all she could feel was disappointment.

At first, Michael couldn't distinguish between the pounding in his head and the knock at the door.

"Someone's at your door." Tamara's soft voice and her abrupt shift out of his arms startled him.

My God! He felt like a sweaty-palmed teenager on a first date. Dazed, he looked at her for an instant before he came to his senses.

"Don't move. I'll get rid of whoever it is," he growled.

This intruder had picked the wrong moment! He yanked the door open with such force it crashed against the cabin wall. Tracy gasped in shock, but Harry held his ground. Jackie's fine hand was written all over this setup.

"Jackie said you weren't feeling well and were having dinner in your room. You look all right to me. What's she up to?" Tracy asked with her usual bluntness.

He deliberately blocked their view into his room by pulling back the door against his side. He didn't want Tamara embarrassed by Jackie's little game.

"Ask my agent." He shot Harry a hard glance. "How did she get the two of you to team up?"

"In Jackie's defense, I must tell you I was on my way here even before I ran into her in the lounge. I had no idea you weren't feeling well, Mike, until I overheard her talking to Tracy," Harry said.

For the first time in their relationship, he wasn't sure he could believe Harry. Harry had been pretty thick with Jackie ever since he'd become her agent. Yet he couldn't quite believe Harry would choose her over him after their long-standing partnership. Something must have showed on his face because Harry punched him in the shoulder and laughed, suddenly his old self.

"I've got a new offer from the network. Honest." He raised a thick sheaf of papers and waved them in Michael's face.

Michael didn't feel up to arguing so he gave in, none too gracefully. "Okay, Jackie's an angel," he drawled, sarcasm dripping heavily from each and every word. "But as you can both see, I'm not sick. And I'm not in the mood to discuss business." He started to close the door.

"Excuse me." Tamara's soft voice broke in.

He registered the shock on Tracy's face and the knowing look on Harry's. Damn Jackie!

A lingering sense of incompleteness, that he needed to know more about her, listen to her hopes, soothe away all her fears, made him reluctant to push open the door. His guts were twisting into knots.

Tamara, on the other hand, looked as if the last few moments had never occurred. She wore the perfect cruise direction expression—restrained and polite. Her uniform had been smoothed out and every loose tendril of silky hair pinned back into place.

"Mr. Shannon, since we've finished our discussion of tomorrow night's activities, I think I should be going." Her voice sounded calm, but when he looked hard at her, she couldn't quite disguise the vulnerability in her eyes.

He felt as if a ton of bricks were falling on his head. As she slid under his arm, through the door and out of his reach, he stood there, stupefied.

"Good night. I'll see you all tomorrow." Did the others notice the too-bright smile, the too-lilting tone of her voice? He did. Even though she walked slowly down the corridor, he knew she was running. As far away from him and as fast as she could.

Cold all-consuming fear froze him to the floor, as if he had sprouted roots. He felt ridiculous.

"I want to talk to Mike alone. Goodbye, Harry." Tracy's tone brooked no refusal.

One glance into her weathered face informed him that, three Emmy nominations aside, he couldn't act his way out of this. Tracy could always see right through him. She slammed the door in Harry's face and turned, a peculiar smile touching her lips. He'd have to apologize to Harry in the morning.

Right now, he wasn't quite sure whom he had to deal with—Tracy or Grandma Lily. She had that "mother confessor" look on her face. In either case, he didn't want to have to explain himself.

He wasn't even sure he could.

"I'm starved!" Flinging silver covers aside, Tracy beamed down at the untouched dinner for two. *"Tiramisu!* Where's a spoon?"

She sat in Tamara's seat, digging into her meal like a truck driver on a long haul.

"Not having to worry about every calorie like those pretty young things is the great consolation of the aging actress. After fifty-five, all I need is my personality."

Michael finally sat down across from her, hoping the food would mellow whatever was coming next. By the time she sighed with pleasure, scraping her spoon around the crystal dish to get every last smear of

chocolate, Michael had constructed a fairly suffi-
cient, if not plausible, series of responses to whatever
she might say.

"Our little Tamara has gotten to you, hasn't she?
And it scares you."

Pinned by her knowing eyes, he nodded, despite his
reluctance to admit to anything. "She's a beautiful
woman," he offered somewhat pitifully.

"So is every woman who's thrown herself at you in
the last ten years. Since I've known you, not one of
them has scared the pants off you like this one does.
How does it feel?"

He gave up. "Damn it, Tracy! She's confusing the
hell out of me."

"Can I give you some advice?" She rose and
cupped his cheeks between her thin blue-veined hands
in her signature Grandma Lily gesture. "Don't answer that. I'm giving it, anyway." She let go and
backed toward the door, wagging her finger at him.
"Listen, doll-face, you're one of the good guys and
don't you forget it. If I were thirty years younger, I'd
have tried to snag you myself long before now."

The twinkle in her eyes lightened his mood.

"Don't be afraid to grasp this feeling and hold on
for dear life. If it's real, both of you will know soon
enough. For your sake, sweetie, I'm keeping my fingers crossed."

She showed him both hands, with all the fingers
crossed and interwoven with one another. Then she
blew him a kiss. "Now get a good night's sleep or your
face will look like mine—nothing but saggy character."

Smiling, he let her go without a word. Needing to work off his frustration, he covered the food and rolled the cart out into the hallway. He took off his jacket and hung it in the closet before throwing himself across the bed. As he stared up at the ceiling, the day's events ran through his mind like a movie reel. As if he were reviewing the day's takes, he played out the scene with Tamara move by move.

It didn't help. His head didn't clear; he didn't come up with a plan of action; the ache in his gut didn't go away. In fact, reliving the feel and taste of her intensified his longing. But it didn't clear up any of his confusion. Did he want her because of her beauty, her body? Why did he want to wipe the fear from her eyes?

He didn't even want to think about what might happen next.

There could be no next. Her world was here and his was in L.A. She also wasn't the kind of woman for a shipboard romance—she'd made that plain from the beginning. He should steer clear of her in the future. What Tracy said didn't apply to Tamara; she was too decent for a foray into passing passion. What if, as so often happened with him, that's all it was?

He closed his eyes. Imprinted on his lids was the stricken look on her face. Maybe he could . . . His survival instinct told him not to get involved. It was a no-win situation for both of them. Yet, he couldn't stop wondering who or what had frightened her so much.

Something primal and strong told him he wouldn't rest until he found the answer to that.

Day Five—Trinidad

After a restless night, Tamara spent her morning session with the Diamond Song and Dance Troupe, unsuccessfully hiding her yawns behind a cupped palm. Last night had proved beyond a doubt that she wasn't strong enough to resist Shannon's attraction; now she just had to convince herself to stop lying awake thinking about him. If not, soon she'd be falling asleep in the middle of a shuffleboard tournament, or worse.

She stretched, blinked and mentally gave herself a shake. "Let's run through the number Colleen and Tony do before intermission," she called.

The entire troupe froze; then every nonessential person disappeared into the wings. She realized suddenly that Colleen, the short vivacious singer, had been missing all morning, although the cast had valiantly tried to cover for her.

She frowned. "Where is Colleen?"

"She's not feeling so hot this morning. Thought she'd sleep in and get better by show time." Tony looked up from his fully extended split at midstage. "Sorry, Tam. I should have told you sooner. Maybe you could stand in for her so the crew can set the lights and sound?''

Damn! There was no reasonable explanation why she couldn't help out. How could any of the troupe know what she suffered each time she got on stage? She turned around and searched the darkened room. The show lounge doors were firmly closed and the rehearsal sign was prominently displayed. Just her kids were here—no one else would intrude.

"Oh, all right. Let's hop to it." She unzipped her skirt and stepped out of it, then shrugged off her jacket. The white leotard she had on would serve just as well for the dance number as it would for her workout in the crew's gym later that morning. She shook off her fatigue as her adrenaline started to pump.

This particular skit required Colleen to ham it up as a damsel in distress before going into the dance number. Out of practice, and not warmed up, Tamara stretched a few times while going over the routine mentally, then sprawled beside Tony on the floor, waiting for the beat.

The start went fine, until Tony softened his tone and began a familiar love song. It had been one of Ally's favorites. She'd played it over and over again in those last few days.

Tamara missed a cue and Tony gave her a funny look, then nudged her. After a few faltering attempts, she began the correct response. By the time her song ended, she'd forgotten Ally, forgotten herself, and was belting out the final notes.

Breathless, she flung herself flat on her back, ignoring Tony's okay sign.

"That's it! Everybody take a ten-minute break!" The stage beneath her shook as the cast members rushed out the side doors to freedom.

Suddenly, a single measured clapping came from a dark corner. The last of her troupe was out the door, and no one else should have been in on the rehearsal. She scrambled to her feet, cupped her eyes and peered into the gloom.

Tracy stood and made her way to the center aisle. "Great performance, hon!"

Embarrassed, Tamara draped a towel around her neck and stepped into her skirt. "Thank you. But I'm a poor substitute for our star."

Smiling, Tracy marched to the edge of the stage. "From where I sat, it looked like you could be the star. Your singing was acceptable but your stage presence and the acting worked particularly well. Ever thought about it?"

"Hasn't everyone?" Tamara shrugged off the question, not willing to dredge up unhappy memories; but the light of understanding in Tracy's face compelled her to continue. "Actually, I did more than think about it once. After college, I went to L.A. to live with my best friend. Ally had already been there two years. In fact, she did a few soaps. Once, she spent two days as an extra on *Another Hospital.*"

"How long did *you* give it, hon?" Tracy's sympathetic smile couldn't be ignored.

"Two years. I left two years ago and took this job. Now my time here is almost up."

"Want to talk about what happened?"

The ache behind Tamara's eyes warned her the memories were too close, too painful to be shared with anyone. Turning away from Tracy's interested gaze, she slipped into her jacket, her fingers trembling on the buttons. "It just didn't work out," she added softly.

"I can tell you don't want to talk about it, hon." Tracy climbed onto the stage and stared out into the empty room. "You know, there's a million stories in this business. Want to hear mine?"

How could she refuse? Tracy wasn't even looking at her anymore. The experienced actress took center stage, her face automatically taking the best angle for the harsh spotlight.

"I've spent my acting life in the soaps. Love every last one of them, bless their corny hearts. But it all might have come to a crashing halt five years ago on 'Bloody Thursday.' At least that's what the cast and fan magazines called it. *Another Hospital*'s producer, thankfully gone now, sent every player over fifty a pink slip." She reached up as if to embrace the light. "Most of us have families we help support, so it came as a real blow."

The earthy voice never wavered but Tracy turned and captured her with a glance. "Mike stormed the head office shouting, 'Grandma Lily is the heart of this show. If she goes, so do I.'" A throaty chuckle rumbled deep in her chest. "Mike does the grand gesture well. So well, in fact, the powers-that-be relented. I didn't get much airtime at first, but I'm a fighter." She took a step downstage. "Got as much out of those minutes as I could squeeze. Now, every week, old Grandma Lily saves some youngster on the show from emotional ruin."

Tracy reached the older woman's side and touched her arm gently. Until that moment, she hadn't realized how cold she'd grown, standing in the shadows. Here was a star, in the business Tamara had been forced to abandon. But Tracy was as genuine as anyone Tamara had met in the last few years and she felt an uncanny sense of rapport with her.

Yet, she knew she had to proceed carefully. "You didn't just happen in here today, did you?"

"Nope. I was looking for you."

"Why?" A suggestion of the confusion and excitement she'd felt the previous night shivered through her.

"You know why, hon. Mike saved my butt. I want to return the favor." Tracy squeezed Tamara's arms, rubbing warmth back into them through the flimsy jacket. "My story's true. I want you to know about the real Mike, not just Stephen Diamond. He's a winner, Tamara. I think you are, too. But you'll both need to work at it."

The room suddenly burst to life as the full houselights came up and the cast reappeared from break. Seeing Tracy on the stage, some of them hesitated.

"Come on in, kids. I'll let you get back to work. The show must go on." Her voice dropped dramatically and she exited with a flair stage left.

Out of the corner of her eye, Tamara saw a door toward the rear of the room sliding shut. For one heart-shuddering moment, she could swear she caught sight of a familiar redhead sneaking out.

Why would Jackie be snooping around here?

Just as the troupe finished the last number, Colleen appeared full of contrition and aspirin, ready to practice one last time.

They walked through her number to make certain the cues were a go. By that time, Tamara was too late for her usual workout and took a shortcut back to her office.

While running down the outside steps to the swimming pool deck, she caught a glimpse of Linn standing deep in the shadows beneath a steel stairway. Her back was heaving in silent sobs. If she hadn't turned at the noise Tamara's shoes made, if their gazes hadn't locked through the steel latticework, Tamara never would have intruded. But Linn's swollen red eyes begged for help.

Blocking the space between the stairway and the ship's bulkhead so no one else could see, Tamara leaned toward the weeping woman. "Sometimes it's easier to talk to a stranger."

A ghost of a smile quivered across Linn's mouth and she scrubbed at her wet cheeks with her fists. "I wanted to have a good cry in my cabin, but it came over me so quickly, I had to duck back here and hope no one could see. They say crying jags happen to pregnant women."

"Congratulations." Tamara tried to keep her tone even, her reaction as casual as Linn's revelation had sounded. "Wayne must be thrilled."

"I don't know. I haven't told him yet." With all pretense stripped away, Linn looked as young as Tamara and Ally must have looked all those years ago.

Hours of soul-searching had built up a barricade that could hold all her regrets of those days. Time and distance were great healers. But ever since she'd come in contact with Michael Shannon, she'd felt those times intruding into her every thought, the regrets, the what-ifs all chipping at her protective barrier. He'd gotten under her skin—him, and the world he represented. She hadn't known what to do back then, how to fight for her friend; how to fight for what she wanted.

She'd never have another chance to help Ally. But with Linn, perhaps she could make a difference.

"Why haven't you told him, Linn? It's obvious you love each other."

"Yes. But he loves his work, too. All of this!" Linn spread her arms wide and then wrapped them around her shivering shoulders. "We've pretty much hid the fact that we live together. We won't be able to hide this." She placed her palms flat on her still-taut stomach and smiled wistfully down at them. "I don't think I want to hide it. I guess I'm more old-fashioned than I thought. I want the whole corny dream." She shrugged as if she needed to apologize. "Marriage, you know."

Tamara stared at the young woman, thinking about what she had to do.

At the prolonged silence, Linn squared her shoulders and tried to smile bravely. "Hey, you must think I'm crazy acting like this. Forget it, okay?"

"I don't think you're crazy. I think you're a woman who knows what she wants." Confidence suddenly surged through her. She smiled, wanting to reassure Linn. "I'm from Kansas, you know. We're practical. If we're unhappy, we fix it. Once we decide what we want, we don't stop until we get it.... You need to tell Wayne."

Nodding, Linn scrubbed the last trace of tears from her reddened cheeks, but couldn't disguise her swollen eyes. "I've been working myself up to it for days. I guess...I guess I just needed a push. Thanks."

Tamara grinned back at her. "Waiting isn't one of my virtues." She offered her sunglasses. "Here, put these on, and I'll engage you in scintillating conversation all the way to your cabin. No one will dare interrupt us."

She could feel Linn gaining confidence with each step they took. As they passed Shannon's door, a shiver ran down Tamara's spine and involuntarily she squeezed Linn's hand.

"I promise I'll tell him." Linn said, misunderstanding Tamara's reaction. "I feel a lot better after talking with you."

Just a few more steps and they would reach the safety of Linn's room; Linn would be clear of prying eyes and *she* wouldn't have to worry about running into *him*.

"I know I have the key somewhere," Linn muttered, thrusting her hands deep into her pockets.

The door burst open. Wayne's cover-boy good looks were twisted with frown lines and his voice shook with worry. "Where have you been? I've been looking everywhere for you!" His words echoed down the long hall.

Beside her, Linn's soft sob coincided with a door opening. She didn't need to look around to know it was Shannon. She *felt* him.

Leaping into the breach, anything to diffuse the tension, Tamara laughed airily. "Oh, Wayne! It's my fault. I kept Linn chatting on deck for the last hour."

"Yeah, thanks, Tamara. It helped. Really it did." Slowly, Linn removed the dark glasses, revealing her ravaged eyes.

"Linn, honey, what's wrong?" Wayne's instant concern, the way he gently pulled her shivering body protectively against him, spoke volumes.

"I guess . . . I guess . . ." Linn faltered before meeting her eyes.

Tamara encouraged her with an eager nod.

"I guess there's no time like the present. I have something to tell you," Linn finished with a great heaving sigh.

Satisfied, Tamara stepped back. Right into Shannon's arms. They closed around her before she could jump away.

"Hello. What's the problem?"

"No problem, Mike." Anxiously, Linn urged Wayne back inside the cabin. "We'll see you guys later. By."

The door shut with a firm click.

"That's the most forceful I've ever seen her," Shannon whispered softly, teasingly, into her ear. "What's going on? Are you giving her lessons?"

Reassured by his playful approach, Tamara allowed herself to remain just a fraction too long in his embrace. His arms tightened and suddenly she realized the danger she was in. The picture Tracy had painted of Michael Shannon had suppressed her natural instinct to fight the attraction she felt for him.

She whirled and studied his face. Obviously he hadn't lost any sleep agonizing through the night as she had. His dark compelling eyes were as clear and intense as ever. Darn the man! Even his skin looked better than hers!

"You seem to be tired," he said softly, compounding the injustice. "Come on back to my cabin. I just had some coffee delivered."

Weighing her choices, she hesitated. To be safe, she should refuse. But she'd never had the opportunity to tell him what conclusions she'd arrived at, even before last night's fiasco; besides, maybe a jolt of caffeine was just what she needed.

She didn't want to admit she was rationalizing, just so she could do what she actually wanted. She'd say her piece and get herself out of there as soon as possible. Then it would all be over.

Finally, she nodded her agreement, and Michael led her to his cabin.

A small cart was laid with a silver coffee service and a plate of her favorite cakes from the pastry chef. She snatched one, munching it as if her life depended on it. She remained standing as Shannon sat on the edge of the bed and calmly poured her a cup of coffee.

"Sit down before you fall down," he ordered, placing her cup on the table next to the love seat.

That was safe enough, she decided, and sat as he poured himself a cup. The sweetness of the icing joined by the hot coffee revived her somewhat. But not enough to give her any confidence when he sat beside her.

He ignored his coffee completely, his hands reaching to gently massage her tense shoulders. "Relax, Tamara. Why do I make you so nervous?"

Her Kansan common sense finally kicked in. Coming here had been a mistake.

She would have removed herself from the mesmerizing diversion his strong hands were providing... except delight radiated from her shoulders and a racing pulse coursed through her body. Why was this man's touch so different from any others? She couldn't imagine letting anyone else caress her like this.

That did it! Despite the pounding pleasure, she finally found her voice. "I came here last night, and today, to tell you to *stop* this."

"Why, Tamara? What are you afraid of?" His warm breath tickled her ear.

When had he stopped massaging her shoulders and turned her toward him? He cupped her face, tilting it toward his. Was she so weak-willed she wouldn't even try to stop him?

She closed her eyes, sighing, trying to remember the last time she'd felt like this. Trying to remember *any* time she'd felt like this.

His fingers whispered over her face, languorously stroking her sensitive skin. Her heart hammered in her chest, her ears, her stomach. She felt as if she were poised on a precipice, waiting eagerly to be pushed over the edge.

One of his hands came to rest lightly at her neck; the other cupped her cheek. Then soft kisses expertly teased her mouth. She was lost in sensation, floating in liquid warmth, being absorbed until she became part of it. She eagerly parted her lips, drinking in his taste.

She hadn't realized two mouths could fit so perfectly. He raised his lips from her eager mouth and gazed solemnly at her until she held her breath in anticipation.

"Where do we go from here, Tamara? *You* tell me what you want." His fingertips played at her throat, making it nearly impossible to think.

Reality intruded and she jerked away from him, panicked, desperate to escape. "What I want... what I need... is to get ready for tonight's fan activities. You should, too."

He stood, towering over her suddenly, and she couldn't quite read the look in his eyes. She felt very small.

"I think these feelings between us need to be dealt with, Tamara. They're not going to just go away because we might want them to." The startling vulnerability in his eyes shook her to her core.

Never forget he's an actor. A darn good one, but an actor nonetheless, her survival instincts screamed.

"I'll see you later." It wasn't a satisfactory answer, but the best she could do with her insides quivering like a landlubber's on high seas.

She escaped from his cabin, but not his words. *I think these feelings between us need to be dealt with... they're not going to just go away because we might want them to....*

"IF I HEAR one more person rave about the blue sky, the hot sun, the white sand beaches, the palm trees waving in a balmy breeze or the gorgeous flowers, I'm going to vomit!'' Jackie complained to Harry.

Quickly checking to make sure no one had overheard, she leaned against the railing. From this vantage point, she was able to keep one eye on Harry lounging at her feet, and also watch the gangway for Michael. She sincerely hoped he wouldn't have the bad judgment to continue his ridiculous pursuit of the insipid activities director—or she might have to do something about it.

Now that she'd overheard that delicious little tidbit about Tamara Hayes's past, she was already formulating a plan. Something had happened to Tamara two years ago in L.A., she could feel it in her bones. The name ''Ally'' gave her just enough to go on, coupled with the fact she'd been on *Another Hospital*. Jackie had her insiders, plenty of little people who would just love to do her a favor. She'd make some phone calls this very afternoon.

She'd already checked the schedule and knew Tamara had the afternoon off. If she tried to leave the ship with Michael, Jackie would come up with something to stop them. Right now, she had to concentrate on Harry, who she sensed might be defecting from her camp.

''Well, Harry darling, have you talked any sense into him yet?'' she drawled, trying to gauge the agent's mood.

''You've seen him.'' Defeat was plainly stamped on Harry's flat face. ''Last night, no one could get a word out of him. He did his bit with the fans and left immediately. That's not like him. One good thing, though, it looks to be cooling between him and Tamara. She didn't even glance at him last night."

"You fool!" Honestly, sometimes Harry could be just plain stupid. Her rage spilled over into her voice. Quickly she gave his shoulder a playful slap to disguise her disgust. "That little brat didn't look at him because if she did, she'd jump his bones. It's very clear to me that she can't resist him. I wish he'd just bed her, get bored with her and be done with it! Then maybe we could get down to business!"

"Then this really *is* just about the show." Harry's sudden animation made her eyes narrow in speculation. He continued, "You don't really want Mike back."

Jackie, who had mastered the art of winding men around her fingertips in the cradle, recognized all the signs. Even though Harry held little appeal for her, he was too valuable an asset to lose.

She slid into her routine naturally. "Harry darling, you know how I feel about you." Fiddling with the top button of his knit shirt, she opened it, exposing his throat, then slid her hand inside. "And you know how important it is that Michael sign this contract. For both of us," she added softly.

She scanned the crowd first before leaning over to put the final knot in the silken strings binding them together. Brushing her mouth over his thin lips, she said poutingly, "You aren't giving up, are you, darling? You know how important this is to me."

She knew exactly how she looked when she pouted; she'd practiced for years in front of the mirror. Harry reacted as expected. A hard mask settled over his flabby face, making him almost attractive.

"I'll get him to sign, Jackie. Don't you worry."

Of course she wouldn't worry. Worry made wrinkles and at this stage of her career, she didn't need another sign of her age. A plastic surgeon could only do so much.

Satisfied for the moment, she turned back to the gangway and watched the passengers disembark. Sunshine glinted off the gold barrette pulling Tamara's hair into an absurdly youthful ponytail, making her easy to pick out of the crowd. At least Michael was nowhere in sight! The two video fanatics seemed to have the activities director well in hand. Good! They'd keep her busy.

She glanced down at her watch, impatience biting at her nerves. What could Michael be up to? Perhaps she should just slip by his room and... At that moment, she caught sight of him striding off the ship.

He was magnificent. His tanned, strong body was shown to advantage in shorts and a knit shirt. A tiny craving throbbed low in her stomach. She knew from experience just how delicious a lover Michael could be. Contrary to what she'd told Harry, she planned to have her cake and eat it, too.

Her appetite was aroused, but she was shrewd enough to choose her time wisely. She hadn't had a threat like Tamara before; it was proving quite a challenge. It might prove entertaining... up to a point. Then she'd move in for the kill.

"MIKE, are you even listening to me?"

Chagrined, Michael turned. In his efforts to find Tamara in the crowd milling around the pier, he'd forgotten about Wayne.

"I'm sorry." He flashed his friend a smile and tried to concentrate on him. A serious twist to the younger man's mouth suddenly struck him as odd. "What's wrong?"

"I need . . . your advice."

The hesitation in Wayne's voice set off a warning bell in his head. "Where's Linn?"

"She doesn't feel very well this afternoon. She's resting." The strain pulling at Wayne's eyes captured his full attention.

"Come on. We need some place quiet to talk," Michael said.

He found an empty outdoor café on the first side street. "Sit!" he commanded Wayne, then flung himself into a spindly chair next to a round table covered with a plastic cloth. There wasn't much privacy to be had with a ship in port for the day, but at least here their voices would blend into the surroundings.

Even though it was early, he ordered two rum and cokes with lime from the hovering waiter. Maybe the strong stuff would put some heart back into Wayne. After the waiter had delivered their drinks, Michael leaned across the small table.

"So tell me."

Wayne swallowed half the drink, probably not even tasting it. Without looking up, he sighed and said, "You know Linn and I have been living together for two years."

Surprised, Michael shook his head. "I didn't know. You've done a good job of keeping it under wraps."

Wayne took short little jabs at the lime wedge with his straw. "You know the rule, even if it is unwritten. Besides, at twenty-four I may be pushing it, but my agent thinks I should try to maintain the teen heart-throb label a while longer.

"Linn quit taking the Pill six months ago," Wayne continued. "It caused her to bloat and she had that diet-drink commercial. You know an extra ounce can look like ten on camera." Finally, he stopped and looked up, his eyes stark in his pale face.

Michael refused to make this easy. Wayne would have to say it, and the telling would make all the difference.

"We're going to have a baby."

"Congratulations! When's the baby due?"

Wayne jerked forward in his chair, blinking at him. "Mike, what do I do? This could ruin everything I've worked so hard to get."

"Bull! You've got what you want." Michael's derisive laughter was all for himself. "At twenty-four, I would have never said '*we're* having a baby.' I knew you thought you loved Linn. But now you've proved you're committed to her."

"I'm also committed to my career. And Linn is committed to hers. A baby screws that up."

Michael frowned. If a woman he loved, and who loved him, carried their child, he knew exactly what he'd do.

A familiar laugh distracted him. Tamara walked by on the other side of the street, her face flushed and smiling at something Joe had said to her.

Hot coals sprang to life, burning in his gut. Unaccustomed to the need that pushed him to his feet, he stood, staring after her.

"Mike, what are you doing?"

He looked back at Wayne. "Let's cut through all the bull. You love Linn. You want to marry her, right? Then do it. *Make* it work, for you, for her, for both your careers."

He threw a couple of bills on the table and crossed the street. Pushing through the throng of people on the sidewalk, with Wayne at his heels, Michael searched for Tamara's golden head. Finally, up ahead he saw her turn to stop at a store window.

"Tamara!"

SHE HEARD his unmistakable voice call her name and stopped as if she'd walked into an invisible wall. *He* was right behind her.

She'd been strolling casually with Irma and Joe, as there was no reason to feel suddenly breathless at the sight of Michael Shannon striding toward her, the Caribbean sun loving every contour of his perfect face.

"Good afternoon, Irma. Joe. I'm going to steal Tamara away from you now." He turned that thousand-watt smile on them.

Irma nodded and Joe chuckled.

"Miss Hayes has been showin' me the mansions and interestin' stuff to tape for the folks back home. The little lady needs a break. Have fun, you all." For once, he put the cap on his camera lens and walked off hand in hand with his wife.

"Making sure he doesn't hurt himself is more like it." Shannon's low murmur made her shake off his hand at her back as he tried to propel her in the other direction.

"I have certain responsibilities, you know." She glanced from Shannon to Wayne. "And what can I help you gentlemen with?'' Her own vulnerability was masked behind a studied professional wall.

"We need to find the best jeweler in port."

Visions of a wedding filled her mind, but she couldn't betray Linn's confidence. "There's a jeweler just on the next corner."

"Great!" Wayne sighed. "I can handle it from here. Thanks, Mike, for helping me see what I really want."

She stared at Michael in shock as Wayne headed off.

He stared right back at her. "You look like you need something cold to drink." Without waiting for an answer, he pulled her along beside him, their hands tightly clasped.

It felt right so for once, she didn't fight it.

The waiter at the small sidewalk café seemed to recognize Shannon. Without an order he produced two tropical drinks. "For you, Mr. Shannon. Your show, best here." A wide grin split the young man's sun-scorched face as he backed away discreetly.

"He knows you?" Everything about the day was beginning to take on a slightly surreal feeling.

A frown narrowed his eyes momentarily. "Wayne and I were here earlier. Maybe the waiter overheard us and figured out who we were."

Curiosity killed the cat, she reminded herself, but her excitement for Linn won out in the end. "I take it Wayne's buying an engagement ring. I'm so glad!"

Her enthusiastic laughter rang out, echoing down the small street. It seemed to have an odd effect on Michael. He looked at her as if he'd never seen her before. She watched a curious mixture of disbelief and something she couldn't quite figure out soften his eyes and curve his long mouth in a smile so potent it nearly singed her skin.

"What? What did I say?" Suddenly nervous, she couldn't sit still. She reached for the drink in front of her. The rum burned down her throat and into her empty stomach, sending out waves of warmth that melted her nerve endings and fuzzed the edges of her brain. She was conscious of nothing but a lazy, hazy delight.

Laughing again, she leaned across the table toward him. When he curled his fingers around her hand, trapping it against the plastic cloth, she felt perfectly free to turn her hand over and reciprocate the clasp.

They sat there for a moment, lost in each other's eyes, entwined hands resting on the table between them. She felt her blood turn to warm molasses.

"Am I wrong?" she finally asked, even though she knew the answer.

"Linn confided in you, didn't she?"

"She's really young." It wasn't an answer, but it was the only one she could grab on to while he held her hand and looked at her so... so...

A flashbulb went off in her face. Then another. The third blinded her, but she felt Michael surge to his feet.

"What the hell! Can't you give us some privacy?"

His angry roar brought her to her feet in confusion. He whirled, whipping her around with him, and pulled her away from the table.

As they fled down the street, the photographers continued to shoot pictures wildly. She caught a glimpse of the waiter in the café doorway pocketing a large wad of bills and talking to someone just out of sight.

Port of Spain bustled with activity. Everyone seemed to be shopping, rushing in and out of the shops lining the flower-filled street. After making sure they weren't being followed anymore, Michael dodged into a haberdashery, pulling Tamara with him.

"I'll take that panama for me and the wide-brimmed black hat for the lady." He slapped money on the counter and rammed the panama flat and low on his head. "Here, put this on."

Tamara shoved her hair under the sun hat, stuck her hands on her hips and smiled at him. She lowered her voice an octave. "A disguise, right?"

His eyes widened in response. "That's my girl!" Then he bent his head, rewarding her with a brief tingly kiss on her mouth. "Now let's get out of here."

By mutual consent they walked swiftly along the street ignoring the crowd and the lure of the shops.

"Where are we going?" she asked, glancing nervously behind her for more popping cameras.

"I still owe you a drink. There must be a bar around here where we can hide out."

She saw that his profile contained a strange hardness. "I guess I never quite realized what a loss of privacy fame brings."

He shook his head. "I know the price and I'm willing to pay most days. But not with you. I want you all to myself."

A curious contentment filled every pore of her body, making her feel too warm, too happy.

They were at a corner when she suddenly heard running feet.

"Damn!" he groaned, catching her hand and pulling her off the beaten track. Halfway down an alley he pressed her into a doorway, covering her completely with his body. The paparazzi thundered by, never even looking their way.

He led her on a twisting route between buildings, through courtyards and down narrow alleyways. She went into her best spy routine, tilting the hat over one eye and whispering with a mock Russian accent. "Where to now, Igor?"

He pushed up the collar of his shirt and glanced from side to side. "C'mon, baby, follow me," he growled, sounding a little like Humphrey Bogart. Except this wasn't the movie *Casablanca* and they weren't star-crossed lovers. Or were they?

They ducked into a walled garden, startling a woman who was pulling weeds. Michael ripped off his hat and presented it to her with a flourish. Hand in hand they went out her front gate as she stared at them in surprise.

Tamara felt like a child again, free and a little wild. They clambered over a low wall that turned out to be the backyard of a church. The small cemetery surrounding a graceful fountain was beautiful and peaceful. Breathless and smiling, he pulled her into the shadows under a low balcony.

"I think we'll be safe here."

She could hardly recognize this Michael Shannon. This glorious man wasn't a fantasy lover or the figment of her daydreams. He was a quick-witted man who made their chase a delightful romp; against all good show-biz sense he supported Linn and Wayne; he had risked his life for both hers and Joe's. At last she realized that at heart he was warm and joyous and generous.

Weakly, she leaned back against cool stone and tried to regain her equilibrium. She was in an unfamiliar and frightening place where something other than the sun burned her and the air was too rare to breathe normally.

This must be how it felt to fall in love.

He turned to her and seized her hand, his face mischievously triumphant. She wanted nothing more than to kiss him.

"We lost them! You were wonderful!" He smiled at her, his eyes brilliant. "I've never met anyone like you." Then, more slowly, he said, "I think I'm falling in love with you, Tamara Hayes."

Every rational thought retreated before the strength of the force beating between them.

"Michael..." His mouth came down on hers, stopping any protest she might have made.

His hands drifted along her body, a tender, reverent exploration. Pleasure built upon pleasure in his arms. Pleasure such as she'd never known. Pleasure that terrified her to her soul.

Then a shadow of reason invaded first Tamara's head, then her heart. Reluctantly, she pulled away. His hands dropped to his sides and his lips stilled their sweet, gentle urgings.

He lifted heavy lids to rest his dark gaze on her face. "You're right. This discussion should be continued somewhere else. Somewhere completely private. Tonight."

"Yes," she whispered.

It was enough to feel his hand grip hers, to have him beside her walking in step the short way back to the ship. Her mind felt riddled by confusion. To touch him had become a thing of anguished sweetness.

At the gangplank she freed her hand from his strong grasp and looked around for more photographers. "I'll see you tonight?"

He slid his fingers into her hair and bent his head, then thought better of it. He whisked one finger across her mouth. "Tonight," he promised.

Her heart banging against her ribs and her blood as thick and sultry as the Caribbean air, she could barely think straight. But she had to pull herself together! There was still so much to do before the show that night.

After checking her office, she quickly showered and changed, taking some care with her makeup and hair. Then she rushed to examine the equipment for tonight's show. She was still on stage when Sheila stormed in.

"The tapes of the four shows the fans voted as their all-time favorites haven't arrived yet!"

At last Tamara realized why the cast of *Another Hospital* walked on tiptoe around the associate producer. Upset, Sheila was a formidable power.

Tamara thought quickly. "We could postpone the event if the tapes don't arrive. Or we could do an alternate event. Maybe have members of the audience interact with members of the cast, in character."

"Very creative, Tamara." Sheila's praise was coolly given, but she went away satisfied.

Tamara went in search of cast members to get suggestions for scenes; hoping, dreading, to find Michael. When he wasn't around, she experienced such acute disappointment it was physically painful.

That pain stayed with her, confused her even more, and kept her from stomaching more than a few bites of dinner in her cabin, where John found her. Merrily, he waved a package at her.

"I think this is what Sheila has been bellowing about all day. She's at dinner and I didn't want to disturb her, so I brought it to you."

Tamara was elated. Now the show could go on as planned and she wouldn't have to worry about keeping the passengers happily occupied with something else. She sent a message to Sheila and went down to the showroom with the package.

The fans began to gather about forty-five minutes before show time. Standing in the wings on the left side of the stage, she saw Shirley and Eileen drag their two pharmacists right up front. Irma and Joe, video camera in hand, took seats to one side where he could jump up to film without disturbing anyone. That was a relief! At least he wouldn't be getting into any trouble tonight.

Tracy and Florence came in, thick as thieves. Tracy was immediately surrounded by fans. Wayne and Linn were already backstage keeping their distance from the excited crowd.

Suddenly, Michael appeared, framed in the open doors at the back of the room. The depth of the showroom and more than a hundred talking, shifting people separated them, yet his eyes found hers immediately. He wanted her as much as she wanted him! The realization pounded through her, dredging up all kinds of conflicting emotions and an unanticipated surge of hope.

She fought his attraction, fought her unforeseen needs, by walking into the center of the stage fifteen minutes too early. She took a microphone into her hand and began to settle the crowd, reviewing the agenda for the night as well as for the rest of the trip. The stage lights blinded her, but for once she didn't panic. Instead, because she couldn't see him anymore, the tight feeling in her abdomen started to ease.

The production crew scrambled around. Finally, everyone was in place. She couldn't wait to begin. The sooner she did, the sooner she could be with Michael.

She tightened her grip on the microphone and for one frightening moment stared blankly out at the sea of faces. What came next? Trying to free herself of Michael's erotic web, she swung around blindly. Jackie came into view. Her smirk was more than enough dose of reality.

Tamara's common sense rushed back. "And now, are you ready to pick the winner of *Another Hospital*'s all-time best story line?"

Enthusiastic applause and whistles echoed through the low-ceilinged room. Feeling more like her old self, she smiled back at their excitement.

"*Another Hospital*'s associate producer, Sheila Peterson, is here to announce your top four choices. I'd like to turn the evening over to her."

Looking cool and composed, as if nothing as disastrous as a missing tape had ever occurred, Sheila took over with great aplomb. "*Another Hospital* wants to thank all of you for taking the time to fill out and return the lengthy questionnaire you were given. The results are in! But before we show you the scenes you have chosen, I'd like to once again introduce your favorite stars."

After bringing each cast member out to thunderous applause, and having them sit to one side of the stage, Sheila signaled for the huge television screen to be rolled out.

"Now, I invite you to sit back and enjoy *your* favorites. There are monitors about halfway through the room for those of you in the back. And don't forget, we're going to pick a winner tonight."

From her position backstage Tamara killed the houselights. A hush fell over the crowd as the *Another Hospital* logo came on-screen.

There was Tracy as Grandma Lily, a little more sedate and composed, but still full of good advice and practicality. Would she ever be able to see these actors in character again and be able to forget about their real lives? On-screen, Grandma Lily was baking a hacksaw into a loaf of her famous sourdough bread. That scene dissolved to a very young, very new actor playing Stephen Diamond behind bars. He'd been arrested, wrongly accused of being the infamous "right-footed revenger" and Grandma was riding to his rescue. The episode must have aired about ten years earlier by the look of their clothes and hairstyles and the crowd found it hilarious. But even then, Michael had possessed his drop-dead good looks, though he'd been much softer and definitely more vulnerable. After Stephen broke out of jail, he and Grandma went riding off on his motorcycle to catch the real revenger.

Tamara felt mild surprise. She would have thought favorite story lines would be full of romance and sex, not just the obvious rapport these two actors had with each other.

She was glad the room was dark. She didn't have to conceal her awareness of Michael just across the stage; she didn't have to hide from the feelings she felt building between them. A bit forlornly, she wished she had known him back then, back before he'd become an international heartthrob.

He was everything she'd learned to fear and mistrust, yet she couldn't get his kindness and warmth out of her mind. Where were all her vaunted barriers? Where was her common sense?

But it was too late for those defenses to help her. She'd fallen in love with him. Now she had to decide what she should do about it.

Thunderous applause jerked her back to reality. The logo appeared again, followed by ten minutes of Wayne and Linn as the young teen lovers meeting for the first time when Bill saved Bonnie from a motorcycle gang. Their relationship built slowly, over a summer of episodes, and Tamara couldn't help but feel that's how it had happened in real life. The way they looked at each other on-screen was exactly the way they looked at each other in person. If only everything would turn out as happily in real life as it had in *reel* life. Their final scene was on a Ferris wheel, which naturally stalled at the top. The night sky twinkled with lights behind their silhouetted heads. Then a shooting star streaked across the heavens and Bill pulled a trembling Bonnie into his arms to kiss her for the first time. It was pure soap-sudsy magic and the crowd ate it up.

Again the logo flashed, this time followed by clips
of a front-burner story involving Jackie and the man
she'd divorced Stephen for, who turned out to be a
serial killer. In the middle of a particularly intriguing
chase scene, the sound faded, then came back on
louder than ever.

The tape jumped a frame. Then another. Then the
screen went to fuzz.

Tamara flipped on the houselights and went backstage to the VCR stand. When she reached it, Sheila
was already there with the technician. The look on her
face gave Tamara a jolt of shock. No wonder Wayne
and Linn had kept their relationship a secret. Sheila
looked ready to murder someone.

"The damn tape broke! If it had arrived in time, I
would have checked it!" Her clipped words fell like ice
chips into the heavy atmosphere. "Naturally, we had
saved the best for last."

Without being told, Tamara followed her to the
front of the stage and stood off to one side as Sheila
took the microphone.

"I deeply regret the tape has broken and we will not
be able to screen the last of your four favorites, Stephen Diamond and his young love, Kara, on the deserted island when she succumbed to her fatal illness."

A collective groan rumbled up from the crowd. It
reminded Tamara of that first day on the dock. Now,
as then, their disappointment was almost palpable.

Sheila held up her hands for order. "However, I
have an idea!" Her voice overpowered the crowd's
displeasure. "I happen to know Michael Shannon has
a photographic memory. If we can get him to come
onstage, he can do the scene for you word-for-word."

Sheila might appear aloof but Tamara gave her points for PR know-how. Wild applause shook the crystal chandeliers as Michael stepped onstage.

Tamara couldn't miss the look he flashed at his producer, but only someone as attuned to him as she was would feel the strain.

"Who do you suggest I do the damn scene with? You?" He growled through lips curled in a feigned smile.

Turning from the microphone, Sheila motioned to Tamara. "Go find Jackie."

"I'm here, darling!" As if by magic, Jackie appeared onstage, flipping her flaming hair over one shoulder. "I thought you'd need me."

"Not Jackie, Sheila. She's all wrong!" Tracy materialized between them. "Let Tamara do it. She looks more like Kara did."

"Great idea," Michael purred, enfolding Tamara against his side in one silken movement.

Conscious of the crowd's anticipation, and her duty to keep them happy, Tamara was caught. "I don't know the dialogue," she offered lamely.

"You don't have any. All the actress did was lie in his arms and gaze up adoringly. She was dying. Just follow Mike's lead and you'll know what to do." The look Tracy shot Jackie held nothing but malice. "Remember, little Kara was the only cast member to get an Emmy nomination that year."

Tension stung her nerves. The bright stage lights flashed on, blinding her again. She heard the audience grow restless and begin to clap in rhythm.

It was a done deal. She knew what was expected of her.

"Let's do it," she said softly, looking at no one in particular and utterly avoiding Jackie's face.

"Kill the lights," Michael commanded and the stage went dark.

Sheila and Tracy and Jackie walked off as the houselights went down. The audience hushed in anticipation. In the darkness Tamara felt Michael lift her high in his arms. Without sight, all her other senses were enhanced; the clean sandlewood scent clinging to his skin, the strength of his arms and the hardness of his chest beneath her cheek. It overwhelmed all her common sense, leaving simply raw emotion.

"Trust me." His whispered breath echoed through her head and made her heart hammer against her ribs.

When the spotlight hit them, Tamara realized Michael had carried her to center stage. He must have eyes like a cat.

Slowly, he fell to his knees, still cradling her gently against him. If she'd had a script full of directions, she couldn't have done more than gaze up at him. A heavy wave of ebony hair fell across his eyes, making him look achingly vulnerable.

The audience held their collective breath waiting for Michael to begin. Then amazingly, it wasn't Michael looking down at her, it was another man, a man she didn't know, a man named Stephen Diamond. His fingertips touched her lips, making her body feel as if she floated in warm water, waves lapping at her chest.

"Don't try to talk, love. Just concentrate on living.... For us. I love you so much."

Her eyelids drifted closed as he kissed her forehead, but she opened them quickly, mesmerized by his face, his voice. It *was* Michael. She had heard this tone before, seen the look in his eyes before, felt the feelings she was feeling before. And yet, it wasn't him at all.

"I thought I was immune to love. I was too tough. Too smart." His shadowy derisive smile broke her heart. "Then you came into my life. You make me..."

He paused as if he had to swallow back some powerful emotion before it defeated him. "You make me see myself differently," he said finally. "You make me see the world differently. If you leave me, all that will go away."

Instinct made her shake her head to deny his words. Surely the actress must have played the scene that way. Only a stone wouldn't respond to the pain throbbing in his voice and lurking in the depths of his eyes.

His hand caressed her cheek to soothe her and then stayed to cup her chin ever so gently.

"I'll try, love, to see the world through your eyes. To be the kind of person you believe I can be. For you, I'll do anything. You touch my heart, my soul, in ways no one ever has or ever will again."

Something sparked in his eyes, lighting them to ginger. Suddenly, Tamara understood why actors were always falling in love with their costars. This moment was so real, so taut with the emotion his words and touch evoked, she couldn't help but reach up to urge his head down to hers. She wanted, needed to appease his pain.

His kiss seared her lips, the heat radiating to her quivering limbs, and she felt her doubts and fears melt away beneath its power.

Loud catcalls and wild applause intruded on the spell woven between them. He softened his hold, separating them. Dazed, she allowed him to help her to her feet. Because she knew it was expected, she smiled into the crowd and bowed slightly before leaving the stage to him alone.

The audience surged to its feet, demonstrating their enthusiastic approval. She tried to concentrate on anything but the confused emotions roiling within her.

From the wings Tracy gave her a thumbs-up sign. Jackie looked as if she'd enjoy strangling Tamara. Curiously, Sheila was looking through Joe's video camera lens, as if she might be reviewing the scene.

Michael motioned to her to come back to center stage. She did so reluctantly. As she approached, he put an arm around her and drew her to his side, as if she belonged there.

What she saw on his face was no act, and it terrified her.

"You're not afraid anymore, are you?" he asked so softly only she could hear.

A moment like this, even if it had been escalated by make-believe, demanded her honesty.

"Not of you. Now I'm afraid of me," she stated simply as she bravely met his eyes.

Sheila walked back onto the stage, seemingly very pleased, and called for another round of applause for Michael. This was Tamara's moment to escape with as little fuss as possible, her job finished. The audience was delighted and she didn't need or want to stay around to know which scene had won.

She knew there was no contest.

Day Six—Barbados

Even in a crowded port like Bridgetown, the trade winds blowing off the Atlantic Ocean kept the air on Barbados cool and fresh. Michael took a long deep breath as he paced dockside trying to keep his own cool. Two harbor policemen, looking dignified despite their official British sailor's uniforms from Lord Nelson's era, eyed him with suspicion.

Michael smiled to alleviate their concern and made an effort to act less like a caged animal and more like a tourist. He leaned against a shuttle bus that had a *Diamond Queen* Tour card taped in the window. Satisfied, they resumed overseeing the disembarking passengers.

After some judicious investigation, he knew Tamara would eventually be among them because she had shore duty as the ship's representative on this guided tour. She might have been able to elude him last night after that gut-wrenching scene onstage, but this morning she wouldn't get past him!

He had to see her. Everything had changed for him yesterday. She had to have felt it, too! First there was their crazy, wonderful adventure outrunning the damn photographers. She had been irresistible. Then last night.

A mere kiss, and a staged one at that, had never before made him ache like a sex-starved teenager.

Damn it! She even haunted his sleep. He'd spent all night thinking about her, reliving each moment they'd spent together, trying to figure out why she was so special.

He should have recognized that first day in the scummy water that she would be trouble.

Drumming his hands against the bus in frustration didn't help to ease his need to see her. Especially when one of the passengers opened the door to ask him politely to refrain. He resumed pacing at a discreet distance from the watchful police officers, but close enough so he wouldn't miss her.

Trouble he could deal with, no problem. But Tamara had become more than trouble. Thoughts of her were beginning to change how he looked at everything and everyone. He didn't know how she'd gotten under his skin but he had every intention of pursuing this to its conclusion—whatever that might be.

He'd fallen in love in the past. Yesterday, he'd whispered into her silken hair that he was falling in love with her. He'd lied. These feelings bore no resemblance to anything he'd ever felt and it scared the hell out of him.

"Mike! I've been looking for you!" Like a kid, Linn raced down the gangplank and along the dock.

"Whoa!" Laughing, he caught her by her arms, giving them a gentle squeeze as she swayed to a stop in front of him. "Be careful you don't fall and hurt yourself."

She placed both her palms protectively over her stomach and there wasn't anything childlike about the look in her eyes.

"Don't worry. I plan to take very good care of both of us. Which is why I was looking for you." She twisted a band on her finger and showed him a marquise-cut solitaire diamond. "Wayne told me about your talk. I know I'm young, Mike, but if love is what I think it is, I love Wayne very much. I just wanted to thank you for helping make everything right for us."

He'd always thought Linn a sweet, beautiful airhead. Now he began to see what Wayne must have recognized long ago—she was loyal and sincere. Those qualities went a long way in Hollywood.

"I didn't do anything. You and Wayne seem to have a pretty good handle on the situation."

"Now we do, thanks to you and Tamara." Linn glanced back toward the ship. "Have you seen her? I've been looking all over for her."

"What did Tamara do?" He wasn't surprised to learn she'd had a hand in creating this happiness; it seemed she did that wherever she went.

"When I talked to her about the baby and Wayne, she was just so sure of what I should do. It made me see it in the same way." Linn's wide blue eyes locked on his face. "She's so real, Mike. It was easy to believe her. And she made sense, so I did what she suggested. If it hadn't been for her, I'd probably still be keeping the truth from Wayne, making him and me miserable." She threw her slender arms around his neck and squeezed hard. "Thanks again."

He watched her stroll back up the gangplank. The odds on her and Wayne making it over the long haul were slim. Michael didn't believe in forever kind of relationships. But, he'd had a real good teacher. He couldn't even remember his dad's fourth wife's name. And nothing that had happened to him as an adult had changed what he'd learned so painfully as a child. Enjoy the moment and never look back had always been his motto.

Yet, he couldn't help but hope Linn and Wayne had the real thing.

"Michael darling!" Jackie shouted and waved from the promenade deck.

"Damn!" The word slipped out before he could stop it. Now there was a real chance he wouldn't be able to get Tamara to himself.

Harry led the way down the ramp and when Jackie stopped to flirt with the policemen, he came ahead.

"Mike, buddy, when are we going to have our little talk about your new contract?"

For the first time in their relationship, Mike thought his friend's hearty laughter didn't ring true.

"After you saved her butt last night, Sheila will give you anything," Harry said hurriedly. "Just name it."

"I want to direct, you know that. That's the bottom line." In no mood to haggle, he was specific. "I direct an agreed-upon number of episodes per year for the duration of my contract. That's it or I don't resign."

"What the hell's the matter with you?" Harry's explosion interrupted the policemen's appreciation of Jackie. They all turned in unison, inspecting Harry's red face.

"This isn't the time or the place to discuss business." Michael moved away, back out of the sun, to the shadow cast by the waiting shuttle.

Harry followed doggedly. "What's with you?" The muscles in his neck corded, emphasizing his anger. "You've turned down chances to do prime time, miniseries, even a movie. Why become a damn prima donna now? You're daytime's biggest star. Why do you want to direct? What makes you think you even can?"

"Because it's what I worked my butt off to go to college to learn how to do. Because it's my dream." Whatever momentary weakness made him reveal himself vanished in an instant at his agent's harsh laughter.

"You—a dreamer! C'mon, pal, it's me you're talking to. You gave up that crap years ago. Dreams are for dreamers, not doers! Dreams aren't for the likes of us, Mike, and you know it!"

"Did someone say something about dreams?" Jackie swept between them. "My dream is to explore Barbados with my two favorite men. It's so 'veddy veddy' British, don't cha know. We can watch a cricket match and then go for high tea."

He resisted her tug on his arm, then reconsidered. "That's a good idea, Jackie, but I'm already signed on for the tour. Why don't you and Harry join me?"

He knew Jackie well and he hadn't misjudged her this time. She took one look into the bus already crowded with tourists and twisted her lips with disdain.

"You can't be serious! Darling, we'll hire a private driver, of course."

"Sorry, I can't. I've already arranged to meet Tracy." It was a small, convenient lie but a believable one. He urged her toward the open shuttle door. "Come with us."

As he guessed she would, she dug in her heels and narrowed her eyes, searching through the clear glass windows. When she didn't see Tamara, she let go of his arm.

"You and *Tracy* go on and have a wonderful time, darling. Meet me for a drink before dinner, though. Promise?"

He kept his sigh of relief strictly to himself. "Sure. See you both later."

He wanted to get rid of them before Tamara did show. She didn't need any more grief from Jackie and he didn't want any more complications.

He handed his tour ticket to the waiting guide and plopped himself in the seat nearest the door. Crossing his arms over his chest, he closed his eyes pretending to sleep so he wouldn't have to speak to anyone else. He was saving the seat next to him for one person, and one person only.

Finally, his diligence was rewarded. Tamara appeared, looking fresh and cool in a yellow sundress instead of her regular uniform, and shepherding Irma, Joe and Florence into the bus. The others climbed in while she had a short conversation with the two policemen. That suited his purposes just fine.

When she got aboard, the driver shut the door and pulled away from the curb immediately. She picked up the microphone before she spied him, then put it down.

He slid across the bench to allow her the only seat left on the bus. "I've been waiting to talk to you."

"I'm on duty." She softened the challenge in her voice with a polite smile before slipping down beside him.

The pool of sunlight filtering through the glass revealed flecks of turquoise in her eyes. Yes, she was sexy. He'd recognized that the instant he'd laid eyes—or should he say hands—on her in the murky water in Miami. And she was compassionate in all her dealings with the passengers. She had that rare talent to make each one feel special.

But now there was something new. Even before yesterday, he had begun to see her as someone special. Innocent and untouched by all the crap he'd surrounded himself with for years. For the first time in a long time, he looked at a woman and saw a person, not just somebody of the opposite sex. It felt strange and exciting. Heat exploded through his veins.

It wasn't just him, either; there was something different about the way she looked at him, too.

He stretched his arm along the seat back and took advantage of the moment. "Tamara, let's face our feelings honestly. Not run away from them." His whisper reached only her.

"You're right. I give up."

He practically fell off the seat! She was agreeing with him! Now he was more confused than ever. He couldn't think of one thing to say, so he reached across to brush her flushed cheek with his knuckles.

"Behave," she said.

Her soft scold didn't have any force. If he could just think of a way to stop the bus and pull her off the vehicle to have her all to himself, he would. Anything. Any price to touch her again, to kiss her again, to pull her under him and . . .

"I mean it, Michael Shannon," she stated, resuming her stern professional voice. "You have to let me do my job today without hovering over me, trying to distract me and making me nervous. It's bad enough you're here beside me. We'll talk later, I promise."

The look in her eyes told him more than any words ever could.

"Tonight we'll do all the talking we need. Deal?"

"Deal." He held out his hand, took hers firmly and wouldn't let go.

Still sitting beside him, she picked up the microphone again and began to address the tour as if he weren't there. But her fingers softened as he played with them, allowing gentle intimacies. Her voice remained steady and he was very discreet. There was no way anyone but them could know what was happening between them.

Satisfied they were making progress, he didn't push her any harder. He just enjoyed the provocative secret they were sharing.

The Barbados sun beat through the tinted glass, saturating her skin with warmth. Michael's fingers teased hers with soft strokes and gentle exploration down the valleys of each of her fingers.

She was too smart to be so confused. Even calling up her Kansan common sense didn't help her now. There was no way she could have asked him to stop, the sensations he was waking in her were too exquisite to give up.

The microphone crackled, drawing her attention back to her duty. The bus was traveling through Bridgetown past Queen Elizabeth Hospital and the governor-general's residence on its way to Gun Hill. She decided to go with the flow. If she concentrated on her tour, he couldn't distract her just by touching her hand, could he?

It seemed he could. She'd lose her place in a commentary she'd given many times before. Finally, they reached Gun Hill Signal Station overlooking the St. George Valley and everyone prepared to get off the bus. His hand lingered until the very last second, but didn't compromise her.

The moment he let her go, she felt back in control. From this vantage point seven hundred feet above sea level, there was a breathtaking view southwest. She made certain everyone had a chance to take pictures, keeping a strict eye on Joe as he began to wander toward the edge.

"You take care of the others, I'll keep an eye on him," Michael promised, heading toward the mountain's edge. He was right there helping her, knowing before she did what she needed next.

"Everyone could tell last night how fond of each other you and Mr. Shannon have become," Florence whispered in her ear. "It's so sweet the way he's helping you today."

Suddenly, Tamara realized everyone on the tour had a strong suspicion about what might be going on between them. She gazed around to discover that Florence wasn't the only one giving her sly smiles. If they could all see how she felt, then Michael must know, too. Taking a deep strengthening breath of warm air, she got a grip on herself. Today she had a job to do. Tonight she would deal with her feelings for Michael Shannon.

After the appropriate amount of time at this stop, which she spent surreptitiously watching every move Michael made, everyone got back on the bus.

He didn't take her hand again which was a relief.

Or was it?

More confused than ever, she decided to ignore him as much as possible. He might be turning her insides inside out, but she had a job to do and nothing was going to stand in her way.

She'd seen the nineteenth-century plantation house several times before, but being with Michael somehow made it seem more spectacular. On a lark, he mimed a sword fight through the downstairs rooms and out onto the manicured gardens. The tour was enchanted with his playfulness. She was enchanted with him, period.

She might be able to pretend to ignore him on the outside while she performed her duties, but he filled her every thought. Somehow she managed to break free of his spell long enough to count everyone as they reboarded the shuttle for their final destination.

High on a cliff above the Atlantic, St. John's Church glowed a strange golden-red in the late-afternoon sun. Off in the distance she could see dark clouds rolling toward them, and as she watched, they gained in intensity, growing darker and more ominous.

She hustled everyone onto the bus, anxious to reach the ship before the storm broke. Michael didn't say one word to her, didn't touch her, hardly looked at her. It was as if nothing had happened between them. Hadn't he felt what she had felt? Didn't he care?

The questions and her confusion occupied her all the way across the island. But when they stood on the promenade deck watching the sailors prepare the ship for departure, she couldn't resist turning to him, a little angry. "You hardly said a word all day. Why did you come along?"

His rueful smile was warm, making him even more appealing to her, a feat she'd thought impossible.

"It gives me pleasure just being with you. I wish you'd believe that."

A sudden moisture prickled behind her eyes. She blinked and strained to disguise her sudden rush of feelings. "I'm probably crazy, but right now I do believe you." Her voice held a faintly breathless quality that shocked her.

"Meet me later, alone, so we can talk. I know you well enough not to suggest my cabin again, so how about the Library Bar?"

A million men could smile at her, and not one would affect her the way the glimmer of suppressed playfulness in his eyes could. How had he changed? The slightly remote and guarded star in private and the public persona he wore with the fans both disappeared when he was with her. It made her feel off balance.

"I'll be there at nine-thirty, after I get off duty."

"Don't get frightened and run away again, Tamara." His open, velvety gaze homed straight in on the pulse pounding above the neckline of her dress. "I *need* to see you."

From a man like Michael Shannon, the last thing she expected was such a blunt admission of vulnerability. Before, he had made it very plain that he wanted her; but need... well, that held a whole different meaning.

"I'll be there. I promise." She turned and fled from her own sense of urgency, surprised by her willingness to believe him.

Michael stood watching Tamara hurry away from him, hoping that the aching tenderness surging through him didn't show on his face. What had come over him today? Her unassuming dignity had tugged at him from the beginning. Now, whatever the hell he was feeling made him decidedly un-Stephen Diamond-like.

Had he really told her he *needed* her? He couldn't remember the last time he'd needed anything since he was twelve years old. He'd always just taken what he wanted—to the mutual satisfaction of everyone involved—but he was consistently honest with himself and his partners about his motives.

In the last two days, he'd revealed more of himself to Tamara than he felt comfortable doing, and he wasn't quite sure why. For a man used to being in control, it was damn difficult to admit he couldn't stem the feelings spiraling through him for this woman.

He glanced at his watch and frowned. He was going to be late to meet Jackie. He always kept his promises, even if they were inconvenient and uncomfortable.

Vaguely, he remembered this was a formal night. He raced back to his cabin to shower and change into his tux in record time. Sparring with Jackie was the last thing he wanted tonight. He needed to deal with her and be done with it.

As he made his way to the main lounge, he noticed the ship begin to pitch in the high seas. Usually, he could hardly feel the motion of the big ship, so he decided the impending storm must be a doozy. Two seamen were even placing yellow danger signs at all the outside doors, warning passengers to stay inside.

He saw Harry hovering nearby and half a dozen men crowded around Jackie, who sat perched on a bar stool, every curve of her body glimmering in a scarlet sequin dress. A foghorn could have been more subtle. He knew she intended to let him know every other man on board found her wildly attractive, but he couldn't figure out why. Their affair had been fast, furious and predictable. Once he'd gotten over the initial lust Jackie inspired with such admirable expertise, there was nothing to hold him.

If he'd learned anything since he was a naive kid thinking the world held some kind of order, it was that he valued honesty above everything. Even tarnished and beat to hell as it was, he wouldn't give that up. Jackie possessed not a shred of honesty in all her beautiful body.

"There you are, darling." She laughed, deliberately leaning into him when the ship rolled sharp to starboard. "Oh, my, it seems we're in for a rough evening."

Immediately, the man hovering over her cleavage reassured her. She responded with wide-eyed wonder, clearly enthralling them all. Damn! She was good at playing the game. Thank God he was beyond this.

Impatient with her act, he grasped her soft shoulder with a cool hand. "Are we having dinner together, or not?"

"Of course we are, darling." Her smile was all-complacent. She could dismiss her retinue now that he was here. With a brilliant smile, she pressed herself into his side. "Let's go to the dining room. Harry has promised to be a good boy and not talk shop, haven't you, dear?" she said, looking in the agent's direction.

Harry shrugged, daring to meet his eyes with a brief glance. "Yeah, Mike, we've got all week to talk."

Harry could talk himself blue in the face, but Michael knew he wouldn't change his mind. Getting away from the set had been a good idea. In the last few days, shadows of old dreams, long buried, were coming together again. And they were painting a bright, exciting new world he had every intention of exploring.

Suddenly, the ship pitched again and everyone around them gasped. Michael braced himself to absorb Jackie's weight, keeping them both steady and upright. A few of the diners, looking green around the gills, pushed past them out of the bar.

"My God, how do they expect us to eat in this?" She tightened her grip on his arm, distress outlining her face, so she almost looked her age.

"They don't. I'll just get you seated and you'll have to make up your own mind from there."

The ship rocked, settling into an uneven rhythm. The aroma of food struck each of them simultaneously. Harry turned a sick shade of green.

"I'm going to my cabin," he croaked.

"So am I." Although suddenly pale, Jackie controlled herself enough to gaze pitifully up at him. "Take me to my room, darling. I feel positively weak."

"Harry's stateroom is just across from yours. He's going, anyway. I feel like some steak tartare and hot mustard sauce."

She recoiled in horror, latching on to Harry for dear life. "You're such a brute," she gasped. "That's why I adore you so. I'll call you in the morning, when this wretched storm is over."

Michael waited to make sure they were safely on the elevator and the doors had closed before entering the dining room. Tonight, the large, ornate room held only a fraction of the number of usual diners. He knew exactly where Tamara sat and made his way toward that corner. Florence rushed past him with no more than a weak smile, clutching her stomach.

From behind Tamara, the low lights pearled her skin and glinted in her cascading hair. She had on another sequin dress with a daring low back. He felt a stirring deep in his gut. But before he could cross to her, Sheila beckoned to him. Technically, she was still his boss and this was a business trip, even if he had made up his mind to make a significant career change.

He had no desire to wear his heart on his sleeve, so he buried his aching need for Tamara for a few moments of duty. Settling himself into the chair beside Sheila, he lifted one eyebrow in surprise at her half-empty plate.

"I can see the storm hasn't affected you."

"This is my first vacation in years. I've even ordered two desserts. That said, you can understand I don't want to do any unnecessary business. So have you made up your mind yet?" True to character, she minced few words. "Your agent is keeping us hanging."

"Guilty as charged. My fault, not his." Prepared to put everybody out of his or her misery, he leaned forward. Out of the corners of his eyes, he caught a glimpse of Tamara gesturing to the waiter. He paused. What was it about her that captivated him so? Her angel face with those green eyes was beautiful, but no more so than many others he'd encountered. Her luscious body, encased in a dress that managed to appear both tantalizing and demure at the same time, didn't explain it, either. It was some inner quality . . .

"What's so fascinating?" Sheila interrupted his train of thought, twisting in her seat to see what he was staring at like some lovesick fool. "I see," she said knowingly.

"Now about the job . . ." He tried to cut her off.

"She's quite a talented young woman."

Suddenly on his guard, wanting to protect Tamara from anything and everything, he studied Sheila, trying to gauge her reaction. But already she'd turned her thoughts back to the show.

"I've got big plans for Stephen Diamond next year."

Resigned, he glanced at his watch. He had fifteen minutes before he was supposed to meet Tamara and that's all Sheila would get to convince him to stay on the show. It wouldn't be enough.

Tamara finished her light dinner and got up to leave the dining room. She knew he was there, had felt him come into the room and was a little curious about why he hadn't joined her.

Just beyond the doorway, she stopped to look back at him. No one in the room was more simply dressed for the evening. He wore basic black with a plain white tux shirt, yet managed to look flamboyantly handsome, catching the fascinated attention of every female in the room. And he always carried himself in a way that suggested he could be out of those formal clothes in the blink of an eye.

That thought thickened her blood and upped her pulse rate.

As if he felt her watching him, he looked up and smiled at her. The intimacy and promise in the lazy curl to his mouth made her back up two steps and bump into someone.

"There you are, Tamara! I've been looking for you."

Twirling around, she was surprised to find Linn. For a pregnant woman, she looked surprisingly hardy compared to the dozens of passengers succumbing to seasickness all around them.

"You look wonderful. Where's Wayne?"

"He's gone to bed. I put a cold cloth on his head and got out of there. He's just a bear when he's sick." Linn thrust out her hand, wiggling her fingers. "I've been dying to show you this."

Tamara sucked in a breath of amazement. The ring was dazzling! "When's the wedding?"

"That's the problem." Linn frowned as she twisted the ring around to hide it in her palm. "I wish it could be right now. I'm only four weeks pregnant. If we could get married immediately, maybe those scandal rags wouldn't be counting on their fingers and having the whole country do the same." She laughed softly. "I guess I'm more old-fashioned than I thought, but I can't help but think of my mother."

For just a second, Tamara flashed to Ally's mom's face when she'd had to break the news. Maybe helping Linn and Wayne had taken some of the pain out of her memories, for she was able to push that picture away immediately and concentrate on a new idea suddenly flashing at the back of her mind.

"You know, people *have* gotten married on these cruises. Ship's captains can't officiate any longer, but there are clergymen on the various islands who could marry you." She looked into Linn's radiant face and knew she was doing the right thing. "Licenses and blood tests aren't required in the Caribbean."

The light turned Linn's eyes luminous. "Oh, Tamara, could we really? That'd be just perfect! When?"

"In two days we'll be on St. Thomas. I can wire ahead and see if something can be arranged."

"Thanks so much!" Linn's hug was surprisingly strong. "I'm going to tell Wayne right now!"

Tamara stopped by the communications room and left a message for the English clergyman in Charlotte Amalie. She had about five minutes left before her meeting with Michael. Shaking from nervous eagerness, she started up to the Library Bar.

The ship seemed oddly deserted. Heavy seas shook the *Diamond Queen*, and Tamara had to grasp the railing to keep from falling as she climbed the inner staircase. Passing the starboard doors on the promenade deck, she heard a loud clap of thunder. Rain pounded against the deck and the window.

Suddenly, a bright flash of lightning silhouetted a figure out in that mess. Then she noticed the yellow barricade had been moved.

"Oh, no!" she gasped with a sure premonition.

She pushed the door open until the wind caught it and tore it out of her hands. Holding on to the iron inner railing, Irma turned, terror stretching the skin of her face tight across sharp bones.

"Joe's out there somewhere filming the storm! I've called and called but he won't come back."

"Go back inside and wait. I'll get him!" Tamara shouted over the roar, her only thought not to have both Irma and Joe out in the storm.

Raindrops stung her bare back and arms and she had to fight the wind to turn the nearest corner.

"Joe! Where are you?"

The deck lurched out from under her and she caught herself, grabbing a bolted-down deck chair to keep from losing her balance. She clung to it, afraid to go any farther, and kept shouting.

"Joe! Where are you? Come back!"

A bright yellow slicker appeared from the gloom. Without a thought to his own safety, Joe was filming, part of the slicker blocking his sight, but protecting his precious camera.

"Joe, thank goodness!" she said in relief. "We've got to get inside. It's dangerous out here!"

"Sorry," he muttered under his breath sheepishly. "Here, let me help you."

He reached for her arm but the ship dived through a wave and bucked like a horse. He fell against her, the sharp edge of the camera bruising her ribs.

"I'm rightly sorry." He tried to straighten up, but couldn't until Tamara braced her feet and pushed at him.

"Hang on to the corner and pull yourself around to the door!" she shouted, shivering from the wind and rain.

Grasping his video camera with one hand, he used the other to grab hold of the corner. The wind fought him every inch of the way. She placed both palms flat on his back and gave him the push he needed to make it clear.

Swaying precariously, she reached for the same hold. A strong whipping wind tossed her back. She twisted, frantically grabbing for anything solid.

A strong arm came out of nowhere to drag her to safety. She turned her head and just like the first time, gazed at him through wet scraggling hair covering her eyes. Instinct made her raise her arms and cling to him for dear life.

Absurdly, she wondered if she could be too heavy for him. Could sequins expand and soak up water like a sponge? But his powerful arms had no trouble with her or the storm. He swept her around the corner, through the door and right past Joe and Irma without a word.

Shock combined with her chattering teeth and chilled flesh kept her silent all the way to his cabin. He stood her up against the wall, minus one gold shoe, with rain puddling from every sequin all over his carpet, and surveyed her, his face hard as granite.

"Are you crazy?" His eyes blazed like hot coals. He reached for her and sank his fingers into her upper arms as if he'd never let her go. "You could have been killed out there!"

The air between them sizzled with emotion. Irrationally, that exasperated her. "Pardon me, but I was only doing my job." She pulled free of his hands and tried to stalk across the cabin, but ended up staggering with only one shoe on. She kicked it off. "What about you? You could just as easily have been hurt. You don't always have to play the role of hero. This is for real, Michael Shannon, not your usual playacting."

A white line formed around his long mouth. "Damn it, Tamara, I know the difference! I leave my acting for the soundstage. Everyone knows and accepts that but you."

"Were you acting last night?" Maybe it was all the emotion pounding between them. Maybe it was the fear she'd felt just now for Joe, for herself, for Michael out in that dangerous storm. Or maybe it was the odd fury at the feelings ripping her apart that made her need to know the truth. Now. This very minute. Her last barricade fell and she looked deep into his eyes. "You kissed me like you loved me, and convinced half the room of it. What part of that was real, Michael?"

A hush fell between them, then his eyes widened and lightened to chocolate brown.

"You kissed me the same way," he said quietly.

Everything dissolved around her in a blinding blaze of stunned recognition. Suddenly terrified of her feelings, she gave one last feeble try at saving her sanity.

"No," she said brokenly, straining away from his silken hands.

"Yes," he breathed and jerked her up against his body.

Tamara could feel each rib above his tight stomach and hard thighs press through his clammy clothes, outlining every sequin into her shivering flesh. Even so, her body melted into his, refusing to obey every rational argument she gave it.

"Yes."

Instinct demanded that she meet his lips with a moist kiss that sent flames licking through her body. Whatever this madness cost, she would gladly pay the price.

She opened her eyes and looked into his face without fear. There was hard desire sculpted across his features, followed by a dawning realization that fed her fire.

His long fingers released the clasps at the back of her ruined evening gown and the soaked sequins fell heavily around her bare feet, revealing her body except for that part of her covered by lacy bikini briefs. His eyes never left her face.

"Kiss me like you did last night," he said.

His voice, honeyed and low, invited rather than demanded. She wanted to respond but couldn't find the right words. These feelings were too new, too endless to limit with mere words. So she took his head between her hands and kissed him, an openmouthed, lingering kiss that left no doubt of her desire. She had stopped fighting herself; and in taking what she wanted, a low moan emanated from the back of her throat.

Michael kissed like no man she had ever known. He kissed as if her mouth were so precious it must be worshiped with his tongue, his lips, his teeth, his scotch-scented breath.

She burrowed into his embrace, aroused by the rough clothes against her nakedness. So completely exposed to his eyes and touch, she should have been shy; instead, she felt free.

Without words, he gathered her up in his arms, holding her tightly against him for a few moments before carrying her to the bed.

"Don't be afraid, Tamara. I'll take care of you." His soft whisper was pressed to the pulse pounding at her throat, making her feel cherished in a way that was intensely stirring. She trembled when he turned away.

Mere seconds passed, then his clothes scattered around him on the floor and he kept his promise to protect them both.

He turned to her, his body gloriously displayed, all sleek muscle knitted to perfect bone formation. All coherent thought fled as he leaned over her, the scent of him dizzying her senses. As she looked up into his face, the moment seemed too exquisite to be real.

Her world narrowed to this bed—to Michael. Michael sinking into the covers beside her, murmuring words of love, sexy words. Michael rolling her gently back and gliding the lacy briefs from her body.

"What's this?" he whispered, brushing his fingers over the bruise already forming from Joe's video camera jamming into her ribs.

Trembling, she tried to find her voice. "I hurt myself . . . Tonight in the storm."

"Promise you'll never scare me like that again," he demanded, pressing gentle, healing kisses on the bruise, making it ache with a different kind of pain.

This time she couldn't speak. She lost track of her breathing as his beautiful mouth kissed her waist, her stomach. A sigh broke from her throat when he at last caressed her breasts with his hands, his lips, his tongue, making her flesh swell and throb with pleasure in his hot eager mouth.

He ran his lips up and down her body until she writhed beneath him, arching closer, wanting more.

She stiffened as he licked her inner thighs, then let out a long ragged sob as he moved down to press kisses at the back of her knees and to her ankles.

Slow, sweet and wild, his kisses went on and on. She was swept out of herself into a mad yearning to be a part of him.

He tortured her with pleasure, yet his mouth and fingers never brushed the one spot on her body still aching to be caressed.

Suddenly, she couldn't keep still, couldn't bear the terrible need. She arched under the pressure of his thighs, wrapped herself around him and rolled him across the bed. Then she spread desperate kisses down his damp chest to his taut stomach, until she felt overwhelmed by the need to taste him.

He moaned, locking his arms around her head, holding her still while he pulsed urgently against her. Caught to his hot hard body she burned, throbbing for what only he could give her.

"Tamara, I've got to make love to you. Now!"

He dragged her away from him and she turned to passionately meet his mouth.

"Yes, now!" she gasped, able to stand the burning ache no longer.

His hips thrust against her and she opened, shuddering under his swelling heat as, at last, he gave her exactly what she craved.

Her body contracted around him and she cried out as the ecstasy built a chain reaction of shattering pleasure that went on and on. This was reality. Here with Michael.

Suddenly, she realized she'd never loved before this moment.

Day Seven—At sea

Jackie knew the moment the storm subsided. Her bed became steady and the *Diamond Queen* again plowed sleekly through the waves. Through her porthole she saw it was beginning to dawn, yet she hadn't slept the whole night. It wasn't the effect of the rolling ship that kept sleep at bay so much as her frantic attempts to put the finishing touches on her plan to separate Michael and Tamara once and for all. Too much rode on his resigning with *Another Hospital.* She certainly couldn't have little Miss Nobody muddying up her future.

She stumbled to her mirror to examine her ravaged face in the highly inadequate lighting. Was that another wrinkle? Ruthlessly scrutinizing every tiny line, she began applying cream and collagen lotion and tighteners to hide them. At last satisfied that she didn't look quite as bad as she'd feared, she began to get ready for the day ahead. There was a lot to be done.

Three hours later, she presented herself in the dining room, starved for both food and attention.

Her entrance could still dazzle a few of the diners, all of whom appeared to have suffered almost as much as she had as a result of last night's storm. Sheila looked up from a plate piled high with pancakes soaked in butter and syrup surrounded by little sausages, and motioned her over amicably.

Seeing that Michael was nowhere to be found, she flung herself into the chair farthest removed from the aroma of the associate producer's greasy breakfast. "Darling, how do you do it? Your cholesterol!"

"One-eighty," Sheila stated blandly. "Would you like something?"

Shuddering delicately, Jackie shook her head and turned to the waiter. "Fresh fruit, a dry English muffin and lots of decaf coffee, black." She glanced around again. "Where is everyone this morning?" When Sheila shrugged, she persisted, "Have you seen Michael? He's usually up early, jogging or working out."

"Nope. Haven't seen a soul from the show. We're at sea all day, so everyone's probably taking it easy."

Jackie decided this was an opportune time to drill Sheila about her plans for the show. She took a bracing sip of the coffee the waiter had brought a moment ago and prepared to have a cozy chat.

"Sheila darling, I've been so worried about the show. You know the ratings have never been as high as they were when Michael and I were together. Perhaps we should discuss my upcoming story line."

The producer eyed her over a forkful of pancake, dripping syrup in a lazy pattern on her plate. "Your story line isn't firmed up yet, Jackie. You know it depends on certain factors."

Oh, how well she knew it! That's why she was on this stupid cruise in the first place. And why she'd coerced Harry into getting Michael to come along, too.

She knew exactly what the *factor* was! And he was being damned annoying!

She couldn't get Sheila to bend a tiny bit, or give her one assurance that her contract would be picked up next month without Michael signing first.

Frustration and annoyance made her seek out Harry. He lay resting on deck in a lounge chair, still looking decidedly green around the gills.

"Darling, you should have joined me for breakfast this morning! They had all those nice gooey pastries that you love," she tormented him. "Have you talked to Michael yet?"

"No." He shook his head slowly as if it pained him. "I knocked on his door on my way up but he didn't answer. He must be around somewhere."

"Then find him and talk some sense into him!"

She twirled away, disgusted. She wouldn't be able to rely on Harry to bring Michael to the sticking point, she'd have to arrange it herself. She went to the health club first, but he wasn't there. Then she took two turns around the promenade deck, but had no luck finding him. She saw all the other cast members and several of the fans who were becoming real hangers-on. But no Michael and no Tamara!

An ugly suspicion began to take hold in her mind. By lunchtime she was nearly wild with jealousy.

The purser offered no help. "I'm sorry, Miss Evans. Tamara is off duty until tomorrow. But I'll be happy to help you in any way I can."

Usually, Jackie delighted in snaring a new man, but her doubts and worries overruled her nature. She had to find Michael, fast, before that activities director scotched all her plans. For some reason, Michael hadn't been acting quite himself since he'd fished that little nobody out of the bay.

"No, thank you." She forced what she knew was one of her more appealing smiles, after a long pause to get her bearings. "I'll wait for Tamara." And how, she would! And when she found the sniveling little wretch, she'd let her have it with both barrels. There was no question in her mind where Tamara Hayes had to be holed up—if Jackie knew Michael. And she most definitely knew her Michael!

Harry lumbered across the lobby toward her. "Have you found him yet? I haven't, and Sheila said something about having new contracts faxed in."

"My guess is that he and our little Tamara are shacked up in his cabin."

He whistled between his teeth. "That's not good. Mike's got it bad for her."

"Oh, but darling, it's really quite perfect. It fits divinely into the little contingency plan I put in motion the other afternoon while you were resting." She looped her arm through Harry's and urged him toward the phone alcoves off the lobby. "Let Michael have his fill of her. It will only make my revelation even more stunning."

She arranged her sundress to show off her long legs and proceeded to dial, then covered the receiver with one flame fingernailed hand. "He'll be thrown so far off balance that we, his old and trusted friends, will be able to make him give up all these silly ideas."

MICHAEL KNOCKED the phone off the bedside stand in midring, giving the cord a yank to pull it from the wall jack. Damn! He wasn't ready for the outside world to intrude just yet.

He'd tried not to fall asleep but it had been useless. Beside him, Tamara slept soundly. He looked at her profile against the pillow; even tousled in sleep, she was lovely, flawless. Her skin looked almost incandescent in the play of shadows and light in the room. Her delicate shoulders were just as enticing as her full breasts, the curve of her cheek just as exciting as the contour of her thighs.

He rose on one elbow to curl his body over her and feel the heat emanating from her skin.

"I think I'm really in love for the first time in my life, Tamara Hayes."

Had he said the words aloud or only just in his head? Should he add that he'd never said this to another living soul, even if she hadn't heard him?

She didn't answer.

She slept the sleep of exhaustion. They'd both been a little wild, making love again and again and again. After their incredible night, he was surprised that just looking at her made him want her all over again. He'd never felt this hunger for a woman before.

An irresistible desire to start kissing her got the better of him. He'd just taste her mouth, breathe in the whiff of perfume still clinging to her hair; he wouldn't really try to rouse her.

His lips brushed hers, and with her eyes still closed, she sighed his name.

Immediately he became aroused. He continued kissing her, unable to resist her petal softness and her sweetness, torn between an unwillingness to disturb her slumber and his need to make love to her again. A shock rippled down his spine when, in unconscious response she slipped her hands up around the back of his neck.

Her fingers teased his ears, threaded through his hair. She flung her head back and wriggled beneath his touch. The dim light filtering through the drapes revealed she had opened her eyes. What he read there, combined with the thrust of her breasts against his chest, drove him a little crazy.

He smoothed her silky hair away from her face. "I've got to make love to you again."

"I know. It's amazing." She smiled sweetly as a long deep sigh escaped her lips. "Me, too."

All he wanted was to lose himself in her once more. But enough sanity remained for him to reach into the bedside table for the necessary protection.

She muttered something soft under her breath and wound her arms around his neck, moving her hips against him. He let go of all his control then, licking and nipping at her until the curve of her breast swelled in his mouth.

Her hoarse cry broke something free inside him. Holding back nothing, he loved her as he'd never loved anyone, ever. For this moment, she belonged to him, and he to her. He held her body between his hands and worshiped each portion of it with his mouth.

She writhed under his lips, lifting her hips to him. Sobs caught in her throat and her fingers tangled in his hair. "Michael . . . please . . ."

He would do whatever she bid. Her mouth opened against his as he dived deep into her hot, wet softness. He plundered her mouth with his tongue, plunged deeper into the secret burning sweetness of her body until reaction rocked him. He tried to hold back, wanting it to last forever. Then she shuddered in waves beneath him as he clung to her.

He'd thought he knew all there was to know about the physical act of lovemaking, but these feelings were so new, he trembled at their power. Over and over they created, both lost in the same pleasure shattering them into pieces to be re-formed as one being.

At last her body relaxed, moisture glistening on her upturned face. She kissed him. Sighing again, she closed her eyes and nestled her head trustingly on his shoulder.

Cradling her in his arms, he could feel his heart pounding, pounding out a new direction. He used to believe nothing could last forever. Now he was petrified this wouldn't.

HOURS LATER, Tamara sat up. Wrapping her arms around her knees, she watched Michael sleep. He was beautiful whether asleep, awake or... Heat seared her skin just thinking about his lovemaking. She forced herself out of the bed before desire overcame better judgment.

She turned the hot water in the shower on full force, then turned it off. She wasn't ready yet to wash off Michael's scent. She found her lacy bikini briefs under the bed but didn't have the courage to pull her wet evening gown over them. Anxiously, she looked around for anything else to wear. She needed to get out of this room scented with the heat of their lovemaking. She needed to get away from him so she could think straight.

His hair was tangled across his forehead as he lay sprawled amidst the covers. Unable to resist, she knelt still naked beside the bed and brushed a heavy ebony wave out of his eyes.

He turned his face into her fingers and opened his sleep-drugged eyes.

"Come back to bed," he whispered, slurring each word.

She kissed his nose and stroked his warm cheek. "I can't. It's tomorrow. Nearly the day after tomorrow." She laughed softly, not wanting to jar him out of his sleepy state. "I'm on duty soon."

He sat up and stretched, pulling her back into the bed, over his warm body, letting his clever hands convince her to stay.

"Let's talk now. We've been putting this off too long. Now that I've found you, I'm not about to let you get away or come up with some lame excuses to keep us apart."

She reached up and stroked his face, teasing her fingers over his lips, silently agreeing with him.

"L.A. isn't perfect but you'll enjoy it, Tamara. Parts of it can be like a dream." He brushed his lips against her palm.

Even that slight caress sent shivers rippling through her.

"I've been thinking about my dreams a lot lately. Since I met you," he said.

He sounded so young, so innocent, she blinked up at him in the dimness. He almost looked like the young man she'd seen on the tape. When had he lost his dream? Suddenly, she was desperate to know.

"What dreams haven't you fulfilled?" she asked softly, stroking his chest.

She didn't hear his sigh, she felt it.

"I worked my way through college by selling magazines door-to-door. Talk about acting!" He nuzzled his face in her hair as though he was embarrassed to go on.

She turned her head ever so slightly and pressed her mouth to the pulse beating in his warm throat. "Tell me," she urged.

"I worked my butt off to get a degree from Northwestern because I was going to go to Hollywood and become this great director. I wanted to be right up there with Coppola, Spielberg, Weir."

She moved away to watch his face. "What happened?"

"Success, I suppose. I got too comfortable. I've lost sight of a lot of things I wanted in my life. Not long ago, certain producers sent out feelers that they were willing to give me the chance to recapture my dreams. I just haven't had the guts to go for it, until now. Until you."

His mouth looked so sweetly delicious she had to taste it. Groaning, he caught her tightly to him.

"God, Tamara, I can't get enough of you. I just want to tear you apart and feast on the pieces," he whispered into her ear before pulling away to lay his head on the pillow. When they were side by side, he looked straight into her eyes. "I've done all the talking. Tell me what you think. What you feel, Tamara. Could you be happy in L.A.?"

He paused and she knew her face betrayed her.

"What is it? Have you been there before? Is something wrong?"

How could she shatter the beauty of this moment with so much ugliness? Yet how could she not respond openly and honestly to the unveiled emotion in his eyes?

A feeling of raw hunger shocked her. She had to put some distance and time between the wonderful truths she'd felt in his arms and the ugliness in her past that she still had to tell him. This wasn't the time for those revelations; nothing should destroy the wonderful glow in his eyes or the feelings springing to life between them.

"No, I haven't been there. Nothing's wrong, Michael." She sighed at her lie, but right now she sensed his vulnerability and needed to protect him. "All my dreams have changed since I met you. But I need to keep my job, at least for the next week, so I have to go."

Anything, any excuse to get away from her lie. Somehow she escaped his eager arms. Despite its cold clammy roughness, she pulled on her dress. Watching his face, she backed away from him all the way to the door.

"Tomorrow?" The question he called out softly was its own answer and they both knew it.

She quietly shut his door behind her and began to shake with reaction. Once, the price of her dreams had been too high. She'd let them all go. Now, with him, she had no limits, and that realization terrified her. She wouldn't survive letting this dream go.

Day Eight—St. Maarten

Michael buried his face in the pillow, hugging it to his body. It smelled of Tamara: her hair, her perfume, her body. An insistent need demanded her presence, here beside him. Damn! Why had he let her go?

Had he imagined it all? He jumped out of his warm bed into a cold shower. The blast of water cleared his head. Tamara was real. What they'd shared was real. And what he felt was real.

Soon he would see her, touch her and feel again these new sensations. He had his dream back. He had a woman beside him whom he loved in ways he'd never believed possible. Now, he did have it all.

Unfortunately, when he opened his cabin door, Harry was leaning against the wall as if he'd been waiting for quite a while and wouldn't be put off. He frowned at Harry, not wanting him or anything else to stop him from finding Tamara right now.

"You feeling better today, Mike? We all missed you yesterday."

"Yeah, well, the storm got to me." Protecting Tamara and preserving their privacy came to him as naturally as breathing. "What's up?"

"Just want to apologize for the other day." Harry had to run to keep up with him as he strode quickly toward the lobby. "We need to settle things, Mike, one way or the other."

"I've made up my mind." He stopped to smile at his old friend. "You know me pretty well, Harry, but you got one thing wrong. I *am* a dreamer. I'd just forgotten. And you know what?" His excitement and happiness came out in a burst of laughter. "Sometimes, a dream honest-to-God comes true."

Harry's mouth fell open in shock. Mike decided it would take a while for his agent to get used to this fresh outlook. He walked away, whistling, hardly believing it himself!

A small part of him still struggled, niggling doubts taunting him with the idea he'd let his glands color his vision. No woman could be as perfect, as open and loving, as Tamara seemed. But he pushed all those fears away, believing that when he saw her again, all would be right.

He reached her office in record time but she wasn't there. Her assistant showed up as he wrote a note on her desk.

"Where's Miss Hayes?" he asked quickly, impatience biting at his nerves.

"She's left for the island tour. If you hurry, you might be able to catch her."

"Damn it! Not again!" The woman looked shocked at his disgruntled murmur, but he didn't bother to explain. He raced through the ship and arrived on the pier just as one bus pulled away. The second bus had already closed its door but he banged on the glass demanding entrance.

The purser's ruddy face appeared at the window. He recognized the noisy, demanding passenger and signaled the door to be opened, a sly smile on his face.

"You're just in time, Mr. Shannon. Take a seat. Miss Hayes is on the bus ahead of us. We'll catch up to them at our first stop."

Accustomed to playing a role, he hid his chagrin at being so transparent. Smiling, he greeted everyone as he made his way down the aisle to the rear of the bus. He sank into the only vacant seat, next to the white-haired fan Tracy had befriended. The bus took off with a lurch.

"Good morning, Florence. Do you mind if I join you?"

"Of course not, Mr. Shannon. But I'm sorry you missed Tamara. She's on the first bus."

Did everyone know? Suddenly, her sharp eyes reminded him of Tracy's. She wouldn't miss much, either! No wonder the two women had become friends. At least, he could talk to Florence without fear of her getting star-struck—Tracy would never stand for that kind of nonsense.

"How long to our first stop?" he asked.

She chuckled at his unvarnished eagerness. "An hour and a half. I'm afraid you'll have to endure a drive through the whole Dutch community. Front Street, the Great Salt Pond. Everyone says it's quite beautiful."

Again he hid his disappointment. Florence kept up a running commentary but it was lost on him. When he gazed out the window, all he could see was Tamara with her head flung back, her hair flowing over the pillow, her eyes glistening as he made love to her again and again. He'd never experienced anything like it. Every time he touched her, he discovered something new, something tantalizing. He hadn't been able to get enough of her, and thought he probably never would.

"How much longer can this damn ride take?" he cursed under his breath.

"Only a half hour more," Florence placated. "Have you noticed the series of dams along the Long Wall? They were built to prevent water off the surrounding hills from diluting the salt pond."

Florence valiantly tried to distract him but nothing could stem the tide of his impatience. He was the first off the bus when it finally halted in Marigot, the capital of the French side of the island.

Holding a clipboard, Tamara was standing in the middle of the square, cheerfully organizing small groups for the shopping excursion and lunch.

Before he could reach her or say anything, almost as if she somehow sensed his presence, she turned and saw him. A smile transformed her face.

He couldn't resist her. He didn't care if everyone was surprised to see him kissing her as if he didn't give a damn about anything in the whole world but her. He was so happy, he wanted the whole world to know.

"Michael, stop!" she gasped and pulled free. A warm blush covered her face, making her eyes stand out a gleaming sea green.

For the first time in a long time, he felt totally comfortable and unconcerned about who might be watching. Tamara had brought about this change in him, making him feel alive again, open to new possibilities. She made him whole.

He executed an overblown chivalrous gesture of apology and the passengers laughed indulgently. Tamara tried to maintain her dignity but couldn't quite disguise her delight.

"I didn't kiss you goodbye this morning," he whispered for her ears only. "I want to kiss you again. Now."

"You're incorrigible." She laughed low in her throat, but backed away in two short steps.

He didn't care about the *Diamond* passengers, didn't know if the other tourists milling about on the street had taken note of them, didn't hear the traffic; he could only feel the surging pulse in his head. Suddenly, everything came together: he was crazy in love with this woman! He wanted right this second to carry her into the nearest hotel room and make love all day. He hadn't felt this way since Stephen Diamond had made him a star.

Hell, he'd *never* felt this way before!

He loved her. Really loved her. And instead of it scaring the hell out of him, he felt exhilarated and powerful in a new way. He began to laugh with the sheer joy he felt, unable to stop himself.

"Michael?" She hesitated before placing her beautiful hands, which had so recently given him such delight, on her slim hips and glaring at him. "What are you up to?"

"Nothing." He shrugged. "You're the guide. So, where are you taking me?" He raised one eyebrow suggestively.

She was shaking with suppressed laughter, but she didn't pull away from him. That was a step forward.

"Smart aleck!" she muttered, then continued playfully, "I'm taking you shopping."

He knew she had to be deliberately trying to drive him crazy by staying with the last tour group longer than necessary. Thank God they all finally drifted away on their various pursuits. She was doing her best to ignore his foolishness, and he was doing his darnedest to entertain her.

Dutifully, he followed her into a souvenir shop. Grinning, he offered her a choice of gifts. White ceramic monkey mugs or pink flamingo sponge hats. When she refused to choose, he bought both.

He loved it. So, he must be in love. Usually he hated shopping and had all his clothes custom-made and delivered so he wouldn't have to go into a store. On this excursion, he spent like there was no tomorrow, buying anything that caught his fancy. Ridiculous gifts that made him laugh. She made him wear the flamingo hat. In return, she fastened a shell necklace around her throat. There was no way he would ever forget this day. The first day of the rest of his life.

At the end of the street, there were no more shops. He looked around in exaggerated wonder, cleared his throat and pulled her up against him. He stroked the side of her bare throat with his fingers.

"Stop it, or we'll have to go right back to the bus!"

She looked beautiful when she was flustered.

"Yes, Miss Perfect Tour Guide," he teased, then dragged her around the corner for a proper kiss.

"Sir. Lady." The street urchin couldn't have been more than ten. Obviously he was the leader of the group of kids gathered around him. "Show you best restaurant in town. No tourists, but all the natives eat there.'' His face split in a wide toothy grin.

Michael lifted an eyebrow. In the States, he wouldn't even consider following a kid to an unknown place, but here...?

"It'll be okay," she whispered.

Holding hands, they went, surrounded by noisy kids. Fifteen minutes later, they were in a part of town that even Tamara didn't recognize.

They came to a storefront with gleaming windows and checkered cloths and no menus. The boy yelled, *"Maman,"* and charged in the door.

A short, rotund woman appeared, carrying a bottle of white wine, two glasses and a loaf of the most delicious-smelling bread. Michael couldn't understand a word she said. He looked at Tamara.

Laughingly, she went into elaborate hand signals, which he playfully mimicked. She slapped his hand down. He tore off a piece of bread and fed her. "Maman" disappeared, chuckling, into the kitchen.

"This is great," Tamara said between bites. "I've never heard of this place. I wonder why that boy picked us to come here."

He leaned over the table and stage-whispered in a mock accent, "Because, ma'mselle, theese is a very romantique place, and you and I, we are very romantique, no?"

She sank into him, her eyes soft. Maman thrust lunch between them—a cassoulet that smelled great. He poured the wine, insisting they twine arms and drink a toast. "To us and our special brand of magic."

As if on cue, a violinist appeared, playing softly in one corner of the room. Tamara looked from Michael to the food to the violinist and shook her head as if she couldn't quite believe what was happening. He couldn't, either, but he was never going to let this moment go.

He slid an arm around her and she placed her head on his shoulder, covering his other hand with her fingers. The soothing melody seemed to float around them, separating them into a world all their own.

"Happy?" he whispered into her ear. Nodding, she sighed.

He turned his head and kissed her sweet mouth. It felt like the first time. A jolt of electricity sizzled his veins.

The door slammed open and the boy appeared. He called to his mother, demanding ten dollars.

Michael gave him twice as much.

Suddenly, "Oh, my gosh, the tour!" She flew out of his arms and grabbed his hand. "We've got to go!"

He left a tip that made Maman blow him a kiss. He left all his crazy purchases with the kids hanging out on the street. Their excited shouts followed them all the way down the street as they ran hand in hand to the bus.

Florence seemed delighted to inform them that John had taken the other bus back just a few moments before. Tamara looked anxious as she took up the microphone. Damn it, he didn't want her to ever be anything other than what she had been today in that funny little restaurant. Happy and content.

"Would you please all number off so I can make sure everyone is on board?" They did, and satisfied, she nodded to the bus driver to go.

She sat beside him, so close he could feel her heat, breathe in her perfume. She looked beautiful. Perhaps a bit flushed, but then, he felt just as surprised by all these new emotions, too.

She flushed even deeper at his hard stare but took up the hand microphone again, ready to do her job.

Thanking the passengers for their understanding, she started telling some island legends. Surreptitiously, he slid his hand along the length of her thigh, tickling her, seeing just how far he could go before she became distracted. She hesitated over some of the story's details but continued in a rushed breathy voice.

Finally, she switched off the microphone. "Will you behave yourself?" The whisper was soft, just like her eyes. "We'll be back on board soon enough." She turned, and one breast inadvertently pressed against his arm.

He heard her soft intake of breath. "I don't want to behave," he growled deep in his throat. He took advantage of her vulnerability by taking one of her hands and playing with her fingers. There was no point in trying to go further. But by the time they reached the ship, he wanted her ready and willing to follow him right back to his cabin.

"*Michael.*" She pulled away and raised the microphone warningly. "What am I going to do with you?"

"Love me." He stated it boldly, confidently. "I've never met anyone who makes me feel the way you do, Tamara." His thumb drew lazy circles on her palm. "I need to tell you so much. About my life, my world. The business can scare the hell out of someone not involved in it. I want you to understand it all. I never want you to feel threatened or confused." His thumb reached down to the pulse beating in her wrist and sketched a heart there.

Her face flushed again and with her free hand she pushed a strand of hair behind her ear. He was content to just watch her, trying to behave because he knew she felt they had to be discreet in public, even though he hungered to plant kisses along her exposed jawline and watch her eyes go soft with longing.

Her sense of responsibility was one of the things he loved about her. Hell, there wasn't anything about her he didn't love! She had altered the course of his entire life.

The bus lumbered along the roads of St. Maarten but he didn't notice the scenery or the passage of time. She stopped her commentary when many of the passengers nodded off from the heat and the effects of their lunch.

"Come to my cabin as soon as we get back so we can be alone." He nearly clenched his teeth in frustration. He no longer considered patience a virtue.

"I can't. I have some arrangements to check on for Wayne and Linn first."

She sounded breathless, as if she was disappointed.

"What kind of arrangements?" He felt a hot curiosity; what could be more important than them?

"It's a surprise. You'll find out soon enough." Her smile sweetened with mischief.

Finally, he could restrain himself no longer. He shifted her uniform collar aside and stroked her neck with his fingertips. Feeling her shiver pushed him over the edge. To hell with being discreet!

He pulled her into his arms, taking a slow kiss from her pliant mouth, creating a low voltage that vibrated between them. She pushed herself away, a bemused expression transforming her into the woman he'd held beneath him last night. Her breath quickened, matching his own.

At that moment, the pier came into view or he wouldn't have been responsible for what happened next.

She picked up the microphone to alert the passengers that they had reached the ship and made a few brief announcements.

At least he still had enough control to allow her to finish her job. She waited for every passenger to get off the bus, greeting them by name, reminding them of the night's activity. His impatience grew. No matter what, Linn and Wayne would have to wait!

As they walked up the gangplank, her lustrous hair bounced on her shoulders, drawing his eyes to the shirt collar he had opened. He could hardly take his eyes off her. Anticipation knotted in his gut; he knew what would happen as soon as they were alone.

The sight of Linn and Wayne waiting in the lobby, too excited and impatient to be ignored, plummeted him back to reality. He'd have to cool it for just a while longer.

"I got your message, Tamara." Linn's face glowed with an inner beauty he'd never noticed before. "Is everything really set?"

"Just about. I only have to confirm one thing with the authorities on St. Thomas."

He felt excluded from their secret; jealousy smashed through his usual sangfroid. He shifted his body closer, staking his claim to Tamara in no uncertain terms.

She glanced up and smiled slowly into his eyes as if she knew what he felt. "I have to take care of this. Then we can have that talk."

"Sorry, Tamara. I need a word alone with Michael first." Jackie's brittle voice intruded on their happy circle.

"Why do you need me alone?" He stepped away, not willing to submit Tamara to any of Jackie's usual garbage.

"It's all right." Tamara's hand stroked his back, draining the tension from his taut shoulders. "Why don't you go talk to Jackie. I need to spend some time with Wayne and Linn. When I'm finished, I'll come find you."

The look in her eyes was a special kind of promise.

"Soon," he demanded, raising her fingers to his lips. "I'll be waiting in my cabin."

He felt trapped. Jackie dogged his heels all the way to his room. He slammed the door shut behind her, the muscles in his gut tight as he turned to confront her. "What the hell is going on?"

"Darling, there's something painful I must show you."

He didn't believe the feigned anguish on her face for one damn second!

"It hurts me so much to say this . . . to even admit it to myself . . ." A sob caught in her voice and Michael wanted to wring her neck.

"Cut the bull—"

She held up her hand. "I know you've fallen in love with Tamara." She took a deep breath as if to fortify herself. "So the instant I was sent this, I knew you had to see it at once."

With a kind of fearful hesitation, she placed some sheets of paper into his hands.

Faxes. The first page was a copy of the front of a supermarket tabloid. Under a grainy photo of Tamara and him holding hands outside the café on Barbados, the headline screamed Soap King Falls For X-Actress Involved In Drug Death.''

The rest of the words blurred into a smear of black and white.

He looked up at Jackie, but she seemed full of sympathy. For one heartbeat, rage burned red behind his eyes, but he forced himself to focus and read on.

The story sent him right over the top. He felt so full of rage, he wanted to hit something, or someone! Instead, he crumpled the sheet and flung it against the wall.

"That's it! Those scum have gone too far this time!" Cursing, he walked in a tight circle around the tiny room. "I'll sue, damn it! They can say anything they want about me, but I won't let them write these lies about Tamara."

"But, Michael darling, it's true." Jackie stood in the center of his cabin, tears glistening in her magnificent eyes. "Once I received this, I called a friend of mine and they faxed me the story from the *L.A. Times* morgue."

He snatched the last sheet of paper from her hand, his eyes devouring the words. He hardly recognized Tamara as the young girl in the picture, her face dissolved in tears, her arm held by a policewoman, but it was her. According to the story, Tamara, a young aspiring actress, was pulled into the drug scene in L.A. by her roommate, whose involvement with shady characters ended in the girl's death. As he read, something inside him shut off. All he could do was stare at the words in disbelief as his dream collapsed around him.

She *was* just a figment of longing, after all. She wasn't real. Nothing about her was real. She'd lied to him—over and over again.

"Darling, I know this must come as a horrible shock, however..." Jackie's hesitation vibrated through the room. "You know I have friends in high places in most of these scandal sheets. For the right price, I can suppress this dreadful story before it ever gets to print. And of course, if you don't spend any more time with Tamara, she'll just fade right out of the picture."

Anger and confusion warred with his pain. For the first time in a long time, he lost control. He couldn't speak. He couldn't breathe. He had the feeling something extraordinary was being destroyed and he couldn't do a damn thing about it. His torment became so intense he tightened every muscle trying to blot it out.

He felt his body begin to shut down. Shut her out—the wanting, the need. He'd have to deal with this in the only way he knew.

"Hell, Jackie, why do I care! The network PR department will wave its magic wand and I won't have anything to worry about." His rueful laugh scalded his throat. "I give her credit. She sure had me fooled. Tamara's a hell of an actress, one of the best I've ever seen."

"Oh, darling, you mean you didn't even know she was an actress!" Jackie's long scarlet-tipped hands fluttered to her neck. "Oh, darling, she didn't *lie* to you about that, too?"

Flinging her hair over her shoulder, she took the papers from his nerveless fingers. "Well, then she certainly deserves everything she's going to get! She'll no doubt lose her job for the S&B Steamship Line. They have a reputation to uphold. According to the paper, her friend was pregnant when she OD'd on drugs. Tamara tried to blame some two-bit producer and the whole story blew up in her face...." Jackie shook her head in sympathy. "Rehashing this whole sordid mess will send Tamara back to Kansas once and for all in disgrace. She probably won't be able to find a job until this all dies down. *If it does.*"

Despite his rage, the image of Tamara's frightened face flashed through his head like a neon sign. He thought of all the people on this ship who liked or admired her and imagined their shock when they read this garbage. Jackie was right. Tamara would lose everything she'd built up these last two years.

Part of him didn't give a damn. Let her suffer! The way he suffered. The part he refused to think about made him stop Jackie at his door.

"So, what's the price, Jackie?"

The smile on her face as she turned to him spoke volumes.

"What do you want, Jackie? Name your price!" He bit out the words through clenched teeth.

"I've already paid off the friend who did this mock-up for me. It gets buried when you sign your contract with the show."

Harry had been right. Dreams were for fools. So was love.

He shrugged, letting go of it all. "Deal. Give me the papers."

With a throaty laugh, Jackie thrust the sheets behind her back. "Not just yet, darling. Once you sign, we'll burn them together. Then this whole nasty episode will be behind us."

He stared into her devious eyes. "I give you my word I'll sign, Jackie. You know I always keep my word."

"I know, darling." Blowing him kisses, she opened the door. "Just as I know from my own sad experience that you are unable to forgive anyone who lies to you. Poor Tamara. She doesn't know what she's thrown away."

FREE AT LAST, Tamara raced to Michael's cabin, anticipation and desire making her feel hot and cold at the same time. She passed Jackie on the stairs and the smug look the actress flashed made Tamara hesitate for one second, inexplicably afraid.

Shaking off that momentary fear, she ran along the corridor and knocked at Michael's door. Jackie couldn't come between them. Not after all they'd shared. Nothing could hurt them. Nothing would ever hurt her again.

She knocked a second time.

"Jackie, I told you—" he bellowed, opening the door. When he saw her, his eyes clouded. *"You!"*

She went icy cold with shock. She'd never seen this look from him before, this mixture of rage and loathing.

"Michael, what's wrong?" she asked in a strangled voice.

He stared at her. After a long moment of silence, Tamara began to shake.

"Michael, you have to tell me what happened."

His continued silence made her heart bang painfully against her ribs and she had to take in deep gulps of air to keep her head clear. Finally, she could stand it no longer. "Michael, please say *something*. Earlier, you couldn't wait for us to be alone to talk. Don't just stand there and stare at me like the Sphinx!"

At last he came to life. He stretched in the doorway and stifled a yawn. "I'm tired, Tamara. It's been a long day. What do you want?"

His resigned tone froze her to the core. If he'd ranted and raved, she would have known he was angry at her for some reason, but indifference was far deadlier.

Stunned with pain, she stared at him. How could he turn his feelings on and off in less than one hour? She went hot, then cold. All the reasons she'd been afraid of him, of herself, and all the reasons she hadn't trusted him at the beginning of the trip rushed into her mind.

"I don't understand," she whispered through the knot swelling in her throat.

His sneer was pure Stephen Diamond. "I thought I was making myself clear, Tamara. You were fun, but now the fun's over. That's all there is to it."

His meaning ripped through her, tearing open a wound too horrible to endure. She didn't think, she simply reacted to the pain exploding through her veins. When her palm made contact with his cheek, her arm vibrated all the way to her shoulder.

"You bastard, you used me!" she said, sobbing, unable to hide her anguish.

"If my memory serves, I think we both got what we wanted." He shut the door right in her face.

Petrified by disbelief, she stood staring at that door, searching frantically through the shattered bits of her life. How had this happened? How could she have been so taken in by his lies?

She moved blindly through the ship to her cabin. Surely there was some horrible misunderstanding. He couldn't just walk away from what they'd shared. It had been more than physical; they had touched souls and minds as well as bodies.

She soaked in her tub for an hour trying to understand what had gone wrong. She was woman enough to know she couldn't have imagined the way he had touched her, looked at her, loved her.

He'd come back and beg her forgiveness. He'd smother her with his wonderful kisses and together they'd eradicate all the misunderstandings.

After a vain attempt to repair her blotchy, swollen face, she sought him out. She wouldn't, couldn't, believe he had used her merely for sexual pleasure!

She found him in the lounge, surrounded by friends and fans, having what seemed to be the time of his life. His cheek held no sign of her attack. Yet it would be imprinted on her soul forever.

He ignored her. No one else seemed to notice, but she felt the huge chasm separating them.

She turned to Linn and Wayne, who were sitting next to Michael. They looked ecstatic that the last hurdle to their elopement had been cleared. Tamara couldn't help but smile at their excitement, even though she was beginning to unravel inside.

"So, if you'll just agree to stand up with me, everything will be perfect," Linn was saying.

How could she refuse the plea in Linn's eyes? Yet how could she endure another moment of this happiness? She fought to control her hysterical urge to burst into tears. "I'd be honored, Linn."

"Then it's all set," Michael interjected, not even attempting to hide his disdain toward Tamara. "Wayne, I'll see you and Linn later." He stood, and without a backward glance, strolled across the crowded room straight to where Jackie held court. Without any noticeable effort on his part, a place was made for him, the place of honor at Jackie's right hand.

"Wayne, I'm thirsty. Could you please get me a club soda with a twist?"

Wayne patted Linn gently, making certain she was comfortable before answering, "Sure, sweetheart. I'll be right back."

The moment he disappeared, Linn sprang to her feet, preventing Tamara from leaving the room. "Now tell me, what's going on between you and Mike?"

"He's changed. I don't understand why and he won't tell me." She knew she sounded angry but she was furious watching him charm Jackie across the room. "It's like he's become Stephen Diamond."

"He's suddenly vulnerable, though. That's not like him at all." Linn sat down abruptly and put her feet up on the facing chair, absently rubbing one ankle. "I've never seen Michael happier or more natural than he's been on this cruise. Even Wayne has noticed.

You'll work it out, Tamara. I know you will. You'll find a way."

Tamara didn't want to burst Linn's rosy bubble of happiness, so she agreed despite her misgivings. She made polite noises, but couldn't really participate in the evening's round of activities. Finally, she felt she could leave the room and go lick her wounds in private.

The balmy Caribbean night wrapped around her. Moonlight streaked the teak deck with silver and silhouetted Michael and Jackie as they stood at the railing. Her stomach roiled and she fought a sudden nausea as Jackie's low throaty laughter reached her.

It seemed to her that Michael moved in slow motion, letting his fingers drift through Jackie's fiery hair and onto her moon-kissed shoulders. Instinct told her he was going to kiss Jackie, kiss her the way he'd kissed Tamara just that afternoon.

She twirled away from that unbearable sight, then stopped in her tracks, determined to learn the truth. She spun back.

He turned and his eyes blazed in a fierce glare, revealing he'd known all along she'd been watching. Healthy, justifiable anger made her lift her chin and turn away sharply. Much better to leave the field with dignity, instead of giving in to her overwhelming impulse to shove them both overboard!

Day Nine—St. Thomas

Tamara's eyelids felt as if they weighed a ton. She
stared out at Charlotte Amalie harbor, a beautiful
storybook crescent filled with sailing vessels of all
shapes and sizes. This was one of her favorite ports of
call. And today should have been full of joy.

Instead, she was exhausted from the dark hours
she'd spent trying to understand what had gone
wrong. How, in the space of mere moments, her life
had become a nightmare.

All the dark images of the past had returned to
haunt her last night: Ally sprawled on her bed, dead;
the pictures; the interviews; the police. No one to help
her; no one to understand. Her own overwhelming
sense of guilt. Then there were the questions. Why
hadn't she paid attention sooner to Ally's mood
swings? Why had she concentrated so hard on attain-
ing her dream of stardom that she hadn't noticed what
was going on around her until it was too late? She
hadn't felt this heartsick in two years.

Ally had been taken in by Hollywood's glib promises of bright lights, parties, success—of being part of

the beautiful people. Tamara tried to warn her, tried to protect her, but it had all gone terribly wrong.

When Tamara had left L.A., it was to take Ally's body back to Kansas. She'd wept with Ally's mother and promised herself she'd never go back. There was no one to trust in that life. Better to lose her dream than to live that way.

For two years, she'd been in recovery, learning to build bridges between people. Gradually, the hurt had healed. Then Michael had come into her life and broken down all her defenses. She'd turned her back on her promises and her good sense, and now, it seemed to be happening all over again—the heartache, the betrayal.

How could he? He'd deliberately set out to seduce her, playing with her emotions, plying her with charm and secret looks.

There were no more tears to cry. And why should she? She'd done nothing . . . but fall in love.

While she used anger and hurt to try to rebuild her defenses, part of her refused to believe what was happening. The Michael she knew hadn't been acting a part yesterday on St. Maarten's any more than he had during their endless hours of lovemaking. She would have known if it wasn't real, and never would have given herself so freely, so joyously.

Something had happened. *Someone* had turned him into that cold hateful man she'd slapped. Her tired mind kept returning to one person: Jackie.

She looked down at her hand, imagining the delights of touching him, loving him. She couldn't accept this. She couldn't, wouldn't, let it end like this. Not without finding out the whole truth.

Just making that decision helped her feel better. She dressed quickly, concentrating on the excitement of Linn and Wayne's wedding day, the last-minute preparations and the role she had to play. She tried not to think about Michael, or the fact that she'd be standing across the church from him in just a little while.

Out on deck, a soft breeze played with her hair, distracting her as she fingered fine tendrils out of her mouth. Everything was conspiring to give the young lovers a perfect day. Pastel stucco houses sparkled against the emerald hills.

To her left, two other cruise ships were docked. It would be crowded in port today, the world-famous duty-free shopping area chaotic with eager buyers.

She double-checked the arrangements for the private car and then caught a taxi for herself. By deliberately concentrating on the bustle in town, the spiral streets winding uphill from the base of the Savan, she kept all thoughts of Michael pushed to the back of her mind. There were still some formalities she had to complete before the wedding could take place.

When her car pulled up in front of the historic, centuries-old church where she'd arranged for Linn and Wayne to be married, she decided there couldn't be a more perfect setting. Bougainvillea, hibiscus and orchids grew in a tangle against the white church, their perfume romantically scenting the air.

The reverend greeted her in the doorway, leading her efficiently through all the paperwork, then offered her tea. She couldn't eat or drink a thing.

She went into the sanctuary to wait for the happy couple. Sitting in the old wooden pew, she found the hushed, reverent atmosphere amazingly therapeutic.

She felt some of her tension ebb. At last she sensed she could be genuinely happy for Linn and Wayne, despite her own heartbreak.

Once Michael arrived, she'd talk to him. She would break through his cynical barrier, just as he'd broken down her walls. He'd have to listen here, surrounded by all this beauty and peace.

A dull pain gripped her heart. How would he react today? Would he wear the cool, perfect mask he'd worn before? Would he be Stephen Diamond? Or would he be the real Michael Shannon, the man she'd fallen in love with?

She heard a car pull up out front and went to the door just as Linn stepped out, looking radiant. Tamara fixed a smile on her face and vowed to keep it there no matter what.

"Oh, it's perfect!" Linn gave her a hug.

Wayne pressed a quick kiss on her cheek. "I don't know how to thank you."

"Just be happy, you two." Nervously, she looked around, smiling so hard her muscles tingled across her cheekbones. Where was he?

"I promise you, we will be!"

They said it together, and with such conviction that Tamara had to believe them.

"C'mon, sweetheart." Wayne led Linn into the cool interior.

They looked like an advertisement for a bridal magazine. Linn had flowers woven through her loosely curled hair and the flowing white dress she wore made her look positively ethereal. And Wayne! For the first time, she understood why teenage girls by the millions swooned over him daily. His white Armani suit set off his athletic body and made his tan appear darker, his eyes bluer and his sun-streaked hair blonder.

They were younger than she. Yet they knew they belonged together and had the courage to make the commitment.

At that point, Michael emerged from the car. He looked right through her before turning to help Tracy out. He pulled dark glasses out of his pocket and settled them firmly on his face, no doubt to conceal his eyes, but she recognized the sneer as pure Stephen Diamond. Tears stung behind her lids and she blinked them frantically away. What had happened to the man who had so tenderly made love to her?

She nearly tripped on the step down to him. Catching herself, she laughed in a breathless little gasp. Pretend nothing has changed, she thought, and said brightly, "Hi! Ready to be best man?"

"Ready whenever you are." His manner didn't soften one bit.

"Michael, don't spoil Linn and Wayne's day!" she implored.

He strolled past her into the church without a word. Tracy's encouraging smile didn't help one tiny bit.

He might have been a statue, standing beside Wayne. His perfect body never moved a muscle and the perfect planes of his face never altered during the ceremony. He wasn't affected when tears began to drift down Linn's cheeks and Wayne took out his own handkerchief to dab them away ever so gently.

Behind her, Tamara could hear Tracy sobbing softly. She felt her own knees begin to tremble, but

Michael seemed untouched by it all. She stared into his eyes and it was like looking at a stranger.

What would it be like to marry the man you love? She silently pleaded with him for understanding, but he was concentrating on the carved altar.

After exchanging the regular vows, Wayne gazed deep into Linn's eyes and spoke his own words of love and commitment.

She could feel the tears trickling down her own cheeks, see the emotion glistening in both Wayne's and Linn's eyes, but Michael remained completely unmoved, almost as if he weren't a part of the ceremony going on before him.

She glared at him over the newlyweds' bent heads as they kissed. Damn you, Shannon, look at me!

He ignored her silent demand, shaking hands with the reverend before kissing the radiant bride. He thumped Wayne twice on the back as a sign of congratulations, then turned, ignoring Tamara completely, and whisked Tracy out of the church.

Trailing properly behind the bride and groom, Tamara decided that while neither the setting nor the ceremony had softened Michael's attitude in the slightest, it had changed her. She wanted this. She wanted all the shivering excitement and the not-quite-believable happiness she'd felt with him a mere twenty-four hours ago. And she was going to fight to get it back.

When she stepped out into the bright sunlight, Tracy was taking pictures. "Linn, honey, look at the camera. You can look at Wayne for the rest of your lives."

Michael shook his head.

"All right. Now I need the four of you together. Tamara, come down here. Stand next to Michael. Everybody, smile."

Tamara didn't know about Michael, but she felt like crying. He loosened his tie and stepped away.

"One more. Tamara, you and Michael together."

For just a moment, she thought he would refuse but then he took a step toward her. If looks could kill, she'd be bleeding on the sidewalk. He was very careful not to get too close, not to touch her. She gritted her teeth, thinking that this would be a pitiful shot. As bad as their first picture together. A lifetime ago.

"I'm going to walk back to the ship. See you all later." He flung his navy blazer over one shoulder and strolled away without a backward look.

Lost in their own private bliss, Linn and Wayne were oblivious, but Tracy patted Tamara's cold hand comfortingly all the way back to the pier.

"We'll see you tonight at seven, Tamara," Wayne said. "I can hardly wait to see Sheila's reaction. Keep your fingers crossed." Wayne pulled Linn out of the limo.

She resisted, leaning back into the car when he was out of earshot. "Let me know if I can help with Mike."

Watching them hurry up the gangplank arm in arm, Tracy nodded her head knowingly. "That gal's turning into a woman right in front of our eyes. I'm happy to see it. Now, what can I do for you, hon?"

Pride made her shake her head in denial. Climbing out of the car behind Tracy, Tamara fumbled in her purse for sunglasses. If everyone kept being so sympathetic, she would start bawling like a baby.

"Thanks, Tracy. I'll see you later." The bright, beautiful day was gone as far as she was concerned. She headed to her office where a ton of paperwork awaited completion before she could leave her job when the ship docked in Miami.

Despite her good intentions, she was just going through the motions. Her heart wasn't in it, wasn't up to anything more than a pathetic quiver from time to time to keep her body alive.

Finally, the hands of the clock made their way around to three. She couldn't stand this any longer. She had four hours before the fan gathering, with the surprise announcement about the wedding, to find Michael Shannon and try to talk some sense into him.

It took her almost an hour to search the ship. She walked in and out of every lounge, every public room, including the health club and the library, and took three full turns around the promenade deck without one glimpse of him. Frustration was making her frantic.

But the craziness of running all over the ship like a madwoman didn't strike her until Tracy stopped her. It was her second visit to the card room in less than fifteen minutes.

"What's going on, Tamara? You look practically beside yourself."

"I'm all right," she muttered absently, backing out the door. But she wasn't, and wouldn't be until she cleared this up. Enough was enough! Her little chase could only end in one place and it would take all her courage to go there.

She hesitated about twenty feet down the corridor from his stateroom. Could she do this? Was she strong enough to face him? All she could feel at the moment was a penetrating sense of loss for the completeness she'd only ever felt in his arms. That emerging dream had collapsed around her. Her soul ached with regret. She didn't know how or if she could ever recapture it. She only knew she was older and wiser and this dream couldn't be left behind by moving to another place or trying to live a new life. This loss would stay with her forever.

She had to at least try.

At that moment, his door swung open and feminine laughter drifted out into the hallway. Her heart cringed and she shrank back into an alcove.

"Oh, darling, you've made me so happy." Jackie's throaty laughter slammed into her.

Jackie again! With Michael in his room—the place where she had forever surrendered her heart. How could he do this?

She forced herself to stay, to see Jackie pull him into the hallway and press a kiss against the beautiful mouth that had brought her delights never before imagined. Her sense of betrayal crushed what little spirit she had left.

"Yeah, well, I'll see you later, Jackie."

Blowing kisses, Jackie disappeared around the far corner. Even with the actress gone, Tamara couldn't move. But she must have made some sound, for he hesitated just a moment. And when he turned back to his cabin, he saw her.

He had no time to disguise his reaction. "What do *you* want?"

The loathing in his voice shocked her. What had she done to deserve this treatment, but love him? Every part of her trembled. The air in the corridor became thick, making it impossible to breathe with any normal rhythm. She clenched her hands together and forced herself toward him.

"Can I come in?"

"Why not?" Shrugging, he stepped aside to let her pass.

She stopped just short of the bed and turned slowly to face him. This was the hardest thing she'd ever done.

He stood for a moment looking at her, then pulled the door closed behind him. It shut with a decisive click and she flinched.

She took a deep breath, still not knowing what she would say. "We need to talk."

"Why in the hell didn't you talk when it mattered?" he said, his temper flaring.

This was better; anger she could deal with. "I came here to ask you to explain what happened between us. I need to understand."

The look he threw at her could have sliced the heart out of the blackest soap villain ever written. Her insides knotted in pain.

"I spilled my guts to you and you didn't even let me have a glimpse of who you really are," he said coldly.

The chill in his voice made her shiver. What did he mean? She'd opened herself to him as she'd never done to another human being.

"Michael, I don't understand what you're talking about. I'm who I always was. Tamara Hayes. Your soap liaison for this, my last cruise." She frowned and shook her head. "At least that's who I was before I fell in love with you. I'm more complete now because of you. Because of what we shared. Nothing else matters.''

It might be an illusion or the pure power of wishful thinking that made her believe his face softened slightly, but she couldn't be sure. All she knew was that he moved a little closer and with every step the room grew smaller, the air hotter, and her blood began to race.

A loud insistent banging jarred the whole room, breaking the growing tension as she faced Michael. She shut her eyes, wanting to blot out the intrusion. When she opened them again, he was already at the door.

Jackie burst in. "Oh, darling, I just couldn't wait to share our happy news with Harry. He's finally got a copy of the new contract for you to look at. Now that you've put all that directing nonsense behind you, we can find Sheila and get everything signed all right and ti..." Her voice dropped off when she saw Tamara, then raised to an unattractive shriek. "What's *she* doing here?"

As if a curtain had lifted, revealing the stage fully dressed for the play, Tamara finally got it. First, there'd been that glimpse of Jackie slipping out of the show lounge the day she'd told Tracy about L.A.; and Jackie, again, on Barbados talking to the waiter as the paparazzi clicked away. She was the one who'd made all this trouble.

Michael's cryptic remarks suddenly made sense. Somehow Jackie had found out about her past and told him before Tamara had found the courage to tarnish the perfect rosy bubble she floated in. Now she understood his anger, but she didn't see why he would give up his dream of directing. Why would he re-sign with the soap if he didn't really want to?

She stared into Jackie's blazing eyes and regret gave way to blazing anger.

"Are you and Michael finished?" Jackie cooed condescendingly. "I have some important business to discuss with him."

Tamara knew exactly what she had to do. "I'm just leaving," she answered with the smallest of smiles.

She didn't have too far to go. Just up one deck and forward to Jackie's cabin where the stewardess was preparing the cabin for the night—placing fresh towels in the bathroom, turning down the bed, putting mints on pillows.

"I have a note to leave for Miss Evans," Tamara informed the young girl as she slipped into Jackie's cabin. She shut the door after her, her heart pounding against her ribs. If she wasn't already leaving the ship in Miami, she'd surely get fired for this.

The manila envelope on Jackie's dresser drew her like a magnet. She pulled out the sheets of fax paper and saw the picture of herself doubled over in grief as a policewoman took her away for questioning. Included were the newspaper articles that hinted she might have had something to do with Ally's death, but not the story that cleared her! Tamara sat on the edge of the bed. Remnants of the old horror wrapped their tendrils around her mind, pulling her back to those moments when she'd found her best friend sprawled dead on the bed with a syringe in her hand.

Despair settled deeply in her soul. How could she have shared this story with Michael in those few precious hours in his arms? How could she have tainted their time together with Ally's sordid story?

If she had, would everything be different now?

When Jackie opened her door, Tamara was waiting. "Now I know why he's so angry with me. You showed him these clippings. But how did you get him to re-sign?"

Tamara's calm resignation wiped the shock from Jackie's face. She smiled a smug little smile as she closed the door, leaning lazily against it. "Why, darling, I'm going to tell you because I know the truth will make you utterly miserable."

Her laugh sent icy shudders through Tamara's body.

"You had it all in your grasp." She shook her head, her mock sympathy a travesty against what Tamara was experiencing. "He did it for *you,* darling. He signed away his dream in exchange for my not digging up all this nasty business again."

Shock and hope rocketed through her. Involuntarily, she took a step toward Jackie. Never before had she felt such an urge to strike another human being.

"Go ahead. Do your worst. Michael will never believe you again." Jackie preened, her beautiful face grotesque in her triumph. "He'll never forgive you for deceiving him. You're off the pedestal, darling." Snapping her fingers, she flung back her head in laughter. "Gone and out! Michael can't tolerate lies, particularly from you. There, aren't you absolutely miserable now that you know what you've lost?"

Tamara didn't know how she got out of Jackie's cabin. Suddenly, she found herself out in the hall, staring at a closed door. "You're wrong, Jackie!" she whispered fiercely into empty space. "I *will* get him back, no matter what it takes!"

FISTS RAMMED into his tux trouser pockets, Michael prowled the ship from stem to stern for hours after he finally got rid of Jackie and Harry and those damnable contracts. On one level he knew he was being illogical and stupid. Why should he give up his dream of directing just because of Tamara?

It wasn't the first time he thought he'd fallen in love. It probably wouldn't be the last.

But it would never be the same again. Damn it! He couldn't even lie to himself!

On some fundamental level he had changed. Nothing seemed worthwhile without her.

His pride was bruised and battered at being fooled by what he'd seen as her kindness and integrity, but that wasn't anything compared to the wound to his heart. No wonder he'd avoided love. It hurt like hell!

God, he had started to believe all that heart-pounding romance his show promoted every day. He wasn't the cynical Stephen Diamond anymore. Every youthful yearning, every unfulfilled dream he'd ever dreamed had somehow all become bound up in one woman. He should have known better.

He did know better.

But he'd fallen in love with her in spite of it.

The wind whipped up and the air tasted salty as he sucked it into his tight lungs.

Damnation! She'd gotten to him with her shimmering sea green eyes and her pouty lower lip that trembled slightly when she was aroused. She'd taken him back to the place of youth where every dream was possible and every new day was full of wonder and challenge.

Music drifted out from the show lounge. He should be in there to lend support to Wayne and Linn when they made their announcement and all hell broke lose.

He had to stop acting like a lovesick adolescent. Maybe if he hadn't fallen so hard, if he hadn't stripped himself of his second skin of cynicism, he could let go of his self-righteous misery. He deserved whatever he got for being such a damn fool.

Maybe he should just rejoin the living and stop all this contemplative garbage. He spun on his heel and joined the crowd in the light and noise spilling out of the open doors. One glance around the packed show lounge told him everyone was here who needed to be. Unsuspecting, Sheila sat tucked into a corner table by the stage. She was drinking some fruity concoction with a yellow umbrella and picking cashews out of the dish of nuts on the table. Tracy and Florence were across the room, deep in conversation with the ship's doctor.

Glittering like a fiery jewel, Jackie held court at the bar, surrounded by admirers, the ever-faithful Harry at her side. Her throaty laugh reached him, a calculated seduction just beneath the surface of the rest of the noise. She was on tonight.

And why not? She'd wanted him to re-sign, and she'd gotten her way.

There wasn't any sign of Tamara. When the house-lights dimmed and the orchestra built its music to a crescendo, he instinctively moved toward Sheila's table. He wanted to be close when the announcement came in case he was needed to run interference.

Suddenly, the spotlight illuminated Tamara center stage. Her hair was twisted up in the back so she appeared all cheekbones and neck. She wore a pale lilac lace dress that made her look small and soft. But he knew better. She was one tough lady.

Desire consumed him. He forced it away by grabbing one of the chairs at Sheila's table and straddling it backward, resting his chin on a fist along the wood while he admired her.

Beside him, for the first time in his memory, Sheila didn't have a clue. He couldn't wait to see her face!

Tamara introduced Linn and Wayne. The sight of Linn in her white dress, flowers woven through her hair and carrying a nosegay of white and sterling roses, finally caught Sheila's attention. She stopped picking at the nuts and sat forward, squinting.

"Ladies and gentlemen, we have a very important announcement to make." Some quality in Wayne's voice brought the house to a hushed silence.

"We want you, our fans, to be the first to know. Wayne and I were married this morning on St. Thomas!" Linn shouted it out, thrusting her hand forward so the spotlight blazed off the diamond circled in gold on her finger.

"What the hell!"

The table almost toppled as Sheila lunged to her feet. Michael reached out and steadied it. Sheila's shout went unnoticed by everyone but him as the room erupted in wild applause.

She paused, glancing around, a speculative gleam in her narrowed eyes.

"Whose bright idea was this little stunt?" Jackie hissed, never liking to be out of the spotlight. She pushed her way to his side but he could tell she was keeping a close eye on Sheila's reaction.

"Tamara's." Tracy grinned and winked at him. Obviously, she felt she had no reprisals to fear.

"Oh, really, what a—"

"Great idea!" Sheila cut Jackie off before the fans could sense any trouble, always the consummate professional. "Listen to the crowd. Watch them," she insisted. "I think we've got something here. Let's roll with it."

The crowd's frenzy shook the crystal chandeliers. Cameras popping in her face, and the ever-diligent Joe recording away, Linn took the microphone.

"Thank you for all your good wishes. But no wedding celebration would be complete without this."

With teasing slowness, she lifted the white gown up her thighs. Wayne knelt and reached up under the frothy material to pull down a blue garter as the orchestra played a suggestive tune.

The place went wild. Amid hoots and whistles, Wayne twirled the garter overhead a few times before he sent it flying into the audience.

Michael caught it, and held the trophy up, smiling for the fans.

"All right, ladies, now it's our turn!" Laughing, Linn twirled around and around. She paused dramatically before sending the bouquet spinning off toward Tamara at the edge of the stage a few feet away. Jackie lunged forward at the same time.

Their bodies collided. The crowd gasped. Tamara disappeared, tumbling backward, falling off the stage.

Michael didn't think, he just reacted. He leapt forward, pushing his way through the crowd, desperation blotting out every other emotion.

SHE CAME TO on the floor. Her dress was bunched around her thighs, her arms were flung out, but the bouquet lay still grasped in one hand. She felt the press of bodies surrounding her.

"Get out of the way!" she heard Michael growl.

"Tamara." The ship's doctor bent over her, whispering. "Tamara, open your eyes if you can."

Her eyelids fluttered, once, twice. Then she opened them all the way, staring around the room as though it were full of snakes.

"Tamara, look at me and tell me what day it is," the doctor demanded.

What a crazy question to ask when her body ached from being trampled, and by Jackie! "Who? What? What are you talking about?" She promptly closed her eyes against the pain in her head.

"Don't worry, Mr. Shannon. It's probably just a temporary memory loss from her fall. I've seen it before."

What was the doctor going on about? She was fine! But as the doctor ran his expert hands over her body, Tamara thought how wonderful it would be to have no memory. She could turn back the clock. She could relive the moment when she'd decided not to tell Michael about Ally. It was the worst mistake of her life.

"Tamara, there are no broken bones. Can you stand up for us?" The doctor spoke in a loud voice as if she were across the room instead of right here on the floor.

"I'll carry her." Michael spoke softly but insistently, sounding like *her* Michael. The way he had been yesterday before everything changed. If only she could go back to that time, and undo the damage her silence had created.

She went scalding hot and icy cold as an outrageous idea took root in her head.

MICHAEL SCOOPED her up in his arms and carried her through the crowd, which parted like the Red Sea. Speculative whispers started growing all around the room as he moved toward the door.

He stopped and looked at the crowd gathered behind him. Jackie had murder in her eye. Linn and Tracy started toward him as Joe continued to tape. The hell with all of them!

Didn't they realize Tamara could be seriously injured?

"Which way, doctor?" he said through clenched teeth.

"Take the elevator, Mr. Shannon. My office is just across from it on the playa deck."

Tracy crowded in with them. He shushed her with a look, dipping his head to show Tamara had her eyes closed. He could feel her pulse racing.

Once in the infirmary, the doctor flipped on a large round overhead light in his examining room and motioned for Michael to place her on the table. The harsh light paled her face, making her seem all angles. She moaned as he slipped his hands from beneath her.

"Why don't you send one of the women in to help me?" the doctor said.

Michael gestured for Tracy to come in and then stood just outside the closed door, like the only kid not invited to the party. After fifteen minutes, he couldn't stand the suspense. He began to pace like a caged animal.

At last, the door opened. Tracy came out first, a guarded expression on her face, followed by the doctor. He was smiling. Michael sucked in a huge gulp of air. He hadn't even realized he'd been holding his breath.

"She's fine, except for some slight disorientation that will pass in a few days. She's asking for you, Mr. Shannon. Go on in, but please, no excitement." The quivering grin under his bushy white moustache didn't seem to fit the situation. "Please excuse me. I'm going to have to report Tamara's condition to the captain."

Linn and Wayne came in as the doctor went out. "Is she all right? I'd feel horrible if something happened to her because of me," Linn said, dabbing her eyes with a lace handkerchief.

"Sweetheart, it's all right. You heard what the doctor said." Wayne drew his weepy bride into his arms.

"What did he mean, disoriented?" Michael threw the question at Tracy, who had somehow become the expert all of a sudden.

"She's a little confused about what day it is."

Warning bells went off in his head.

"Just what day does she think it is?"

"She's lost about thirty-six hours. That's why the doctor was grinning at you like a Cheshire cat. Tamara couldn't figure out how she got from your bed to the doctor's office and said so quite plainly."

It was all too perfect.

"Didn't we do this plot five years ago, Tracy?"

Grandma Lily fans wouldn't have recognized the outraged sneer Tracy threw at him. "Why, you arrogant ass! Do you think we all have nothing better to do than pander to your childish behavior! Or whatever it is that's making you act like an idiot all of a sudden where Tamara is concerned. What is wrong with you?"

Wrong! He was being ripped in two and didn't know how in the hell to stop it. If Tamara had really lost her memory, he'd have to live through this whole miserable episode again. He would once more see her anguish when he rejected her. Hell, she'd probably slap him again.

"Mike, my sister was a cheerleader in college. She fell off the top of one of those human pyramids and the same thing happened to her, except she lost a whole week." Wayne stared at him, a frown marking his smooth forehead at Michael's continued silence. "It's a part of having a concussion, but it passes in a few days."

Then the thought came to Michael that he might not have to relive this nightmare, after all. Maybe, somehow, he could go back and fix it. It seemed too good to be true. Just like Tamara. But though Tracy and Linn were fully capable of plotting this scenario, straight out of a soap story line, in some crazy attempt to fix what ailed him, Wayne would never be a part of such ridiculous high jinks.

He smelled a rat, several of them, but there was a slim chance he could be wrong. Considering Tamara might really be hurt, he couldn't take the chance.

"She wants to see you." Tracy nodded toward the closed door. "Just don't upset her. Whatever has happened in the last day or so, she has to remember it on her own."

"Lord, Tracy, that sounds like something one of the doctors would say on *Another Hospital*. When did you get your license?"

"About the same time you turned into a pompous ass!" She shook her finger at him accusingly. "The whole ship knows something's gone wrong between you and Tamara. *That* has nothing to do with this! That poor injured girl thinks she needs you."

The waiting room reeked with rebuke. Even Wayne stared at him, disapproval written all over his face.

"All right, all right, I'm a jerk. So, I'll do whatever it takes to help Tamara."

He stepped over the threshold and deliberately shut the door on his audience. The harsh lamp had been turned off and the indirect lighting cast a warm glow across Tamara's face. There was a bruise forming along her left cheekbone.

For a second he couldn't breathe. It might be true. He narrowed his eyes, studying her. She looked innocent. Innocent and bruised and confused. She looked beautiful.

"I feel so odd," she said as she turned to him, her voice low and tremulous, her lip quivering the way he remembered so vividly. "The last thing I remember is falling asleep beside you and now here I am stuck in the infirmary until morning. Did I miss anything?"

For a split second he hesitated. Then she reached her arms out toward him. Cynically, he decided this could mean one of two things; either she really was hurt or she was the greatest little actress he'd ever come across.

"Don't worry about it."

He tentatively sat on the side of her bed. There was no hesitation on her part as she naturally and trustingly curled against him.

The hell with it! He'd go along for the ride until he knew the truth.

He climbed into bed with her, sliding his arm behind her. She sighed, resting her cheek against his chest. That gave him the opportunity to stroke the injured one with his fingertips.

"Don't worry about it," he whispered again into her hair, inhaling its perfume. "We'll put all the pieces together for you tomorrow."

Day Ten—At Sea

There wasn't one corner of this whole miserable ship where Jackie could avoid hearing Tamara's name, and speculation about her amnesia. Hah! Even Harry had bored her with it when they shared coffee early in her cabin. Trying to figure out what that little nobody could be up to was giving her a headache.

There was even a rumor that somehow Tamara had only lost the last thirty-six hours. Jackie was definitely seeing red. She could almost admire Tamara, as long as this pathetic stratagem wouldn't spell trouble for her own plotting.

Convinced Tamara would never have come up with this scenario on her own, she finally went to the pool to catch up on the latest gossip. Linn and Wayne were having breakfast, surrounded by well-wishers.

And wasn't Linn a sly puss? Even Sheila had capitulated to the fans' overwhelming approval. She wandered around the lavish breakfast buffet at the pool, picking at the fresh fruit and chatting with her fans until she saw her chance when Wayne left the table. Excusing herself hurriedly, she snatched a glass of tomato juice and strolled nonchalantly over to Linn's table.

"Linn, darling, how divine you look today! Marriage agrees with you, it really does." Perching in Wayne's deserted chair, she leaned across the table confidingly. "It's a terrible shame that Tamara's fall broke up your little party. And how is the poor thing?"

"Wasn't it just awful?" Linn's eyes widened innocently. "I feel just horrible about it. We called the infirmary earlier and spoke to the doctor. He said she was still sleeping."

"What about her... condition?" Jackie had practiced just the right look, curiosity combined with concern. "I mean, is it really true she doesn't know what day it is?"

"Yes, can you imagine how awful that must be?"

Marriage must be affecting Linn—a tear actually rolled down her cheek! Jackie was quickly losing patience with all the sympathy Tamara had captured.

"You know, the same thing happened to Wayne's sister in college. He was worried sick about her, but her memory loss was temporary. The doctor told us Tamara will be fine in a few days."

"I'm so glad to hear it," Jackie lied. There was something about this setup that made her radar quiver. The whole thing was simply too convenient.

She spied Wayne returning with a stuffed teddy bear and stood, anxious to avoid the schmaltzy atmosphere hanging over the two lovebirds.

"I'm going to the infirmary right now to see for myself how little Tamara is doing. Enjoy your breakfast, darling."

"That's really thoughtful of you, Jackie. Say hello to her from both of us."

She whirled to hide her irritation. Tamara might fool Linn, Wayne, Michael and the doctor, but she certainly couldn't fool her! She'd persuade the doctor to allow her a peek at the dear creature and when *she* got through with her, there would be no doubts about what game she played.

"Jackie, I've been looking all over for you!"

Intent on ferreting out Tamara's secret, Jackie hadn't noticed Sheila sitting right in her pathway. Her radar really was off today. A shudder rippled over her at the sight of Sheila stuffing herself with every cholesterol-laden goody on the buffet. Really, the unfairness of it made her want to scream in frustration. The associate producer ate like a pig and never gained an ounce!

She smiled sweetly. "Sheila, darling, what can I do for you?"

"I just wanted to thank you for whatever you did to help Mike make up his mind. I got the show to fax a new contract for him to sign."

"Oh, I'm always happy to do my part, especially for the good of the show. Speaking of which..."

Clever Sheila immediately understood. "Next year is firming up now since I've spoken with the writers and told them they can expect Michael back. This could be an interesting season, for everyone concerned."

Visions of another Emmy nomination danced through Jackie's head. She was always at her best when she was scheming to get Stephen Diamond back in her bed. But she knew Sheila didn't like to be pumped or second-guessed, so she made the excuse she was on her way to the infirmary to check on Tamara.

It never hurt to let the powers-that-be know what a caring, thoughtful person she could be. Even though she'd wring that girl's neck personally if this stunt changed Michael's mind about anything.

She swept through the infirmary door in her best "star" fashion. By the dazzled look on the doctor's face, she could tell he would be putty in her hands. But before she could put her talents to work, she got a tingling feeling down her spine.

"Hello, Jackie. How are you this morning?"

She whipped around to find Tracy sprawled in a chair, an open magazine on her lap. Her self-satisfied smile was nauseating. It would be easier to swim back to Florida than to get anything out of her in this mood. No doubt Tracy had primed the doctor thoroughly.

"Darling, you're here to see Tamara, of course. So am I. Isn't it just awful?" Jackie commiserated.

"You'll have to wait, *darling*. Mike's in there with her."

Controlling an overwhelming urge to scream, Jackie smiled. "Oh, of course he is." She'd never let the old bag think she'd pulled one over on her. "How long has he been in there?"

Chuckling deep in her throat, Tracy met the doctor's eyes across the waiting room and said in her sweetest Grandma Lily voice, "I'd say about ten hours."

MICHAEL WOKE UP confused. Where was he? The room wasn't familiar, but the body pressed tightly against him felt right.

He blinked. A dim wall light still burned across the room. There was a faint scent of roses wafting over his shoulder. He stretched, careful not to disturb her, and focused on a bridal bouquet.

Damn! It all came rushing back. Had he fallen asleep for one hour or two?

He hadn't meant to sleep at all. He was only going to hold Tamara until she fell asleep, just to give her some small comfort. He was still angry with her, but as soon as she remembered that he'd dropped her like a hot potato, he could cut this loving act. Except he was finding it harder to hang on to his anger than to fake caring. Particularly with her in his arms.

He couldn't even see his watch because it was hidden by Tamara's golden hair spilling across his hand. She felt warm and soft in his arms. The memories of exquisite pleasures washed over him, tormenting him.

"Are you awake?"

The voice sounded timid. Poor kid, she must still be disoriented.

"Yeah, I'm awake." He shifted so he could see her face. They'd slept longer than he'd thought. The bruise had spread beneath her flushed cheek, making a purple slash against her delicate jawline. "How do you feel?"

"Bewildered." She eased her head back on his shoulder and her smile looked uncertain. "It's really strange that I've lost a whole day. Especially our time together. Tell me how I got back to my cabin that night."

He didn't know how to classify the feelings ripping through his body. He stared at her, speechless. What should he do? Say? He had to be careful while she was in this delicate state.

She squeezed her eyebrows together in a frown as she searched his face. She looked frightened, as well as confused, making it appear her amnesia was real. Could he trust her? Could he trust himself?

"Is something wrong, Michael?"

"You just got up and left." Somehow he kept the edge out of his voice.

"Is that all?" she asked softly, still watching him with worry distorting her lovely face.

He smiled to reassure her, although he felt uneasy. "We talked. About our dreams. Where we've been, where we want to go." He hesitated, wondering how far he should push. "Actually, it was intense. I spilled my guts to you. I wanted you to do the same."

He could feel her begin to tremble in his arms, and somehow that made her seem so much more vulnerable. He would have to be very careful.

"Then, I must have told you about Los Angeles. Losing my dream of being an actress. About Ally."

He felt her go rigid in his arms, felt her tension and confusion as she sought for the right words to explain. Her eyes glazed over and she looked as if she were searching for some kind of answer.

"I didn't even realize she needed help until it was too late. Then I didn't know how to help her. How to help myself. In the end, I didn't do either." She turned in his arms and pressed her face against his. "It's taken me a long time to deal with it. Until I met you. I can't believe I had the courage to tell you that night.

It . . . it must have spoiled our evening." A ghost of a smile brushed across her mouth. "But you know it all, so it must be okay."

Somehow, hearing her brief explanation, although it offered no specifics, made everything crystal clear. But that didn't assuage the pain or the betrayal he felt. She hadn't trusted him enough to tell him the truth when it really mattered; how could he ever put his trust in her?

She started to cry, small silent tears that ran down her face. Michael wanted to touch her, hold her, do something to help her, yet somehow he couldn't. His pride wouldn't let him.

"What I do know is that you've got to take it easy." He slid out of bed, anxious to be physically away from her. "Doctor's orders."

"Will I see you later? If I've lost a day, we must be at sea. Will you meet me later? I want to hear all about Linn and Wayne's wedding."

Angrily, quickly, he backed to the door. *You sucker!* He knew damn well what he should do. But she looked so fragile sitting up in bed, her face smeared by tears, her hair tangled across her bruised cheek, that he did the opposite.

"I'll see you in the dining room at one for lunch." He flipped off the light switch before opening the door.

He felt like putting his fist through a wall. What had gone wrong? He'd won and lost at love before. Why did this time seem so different?

He didn't have a chance to recover before coming face-to-face with most of his costars. Furious with himself, he snapped, "What do you all want?"

Jackie winced, looking wounded. Her lips pouted, very prettily, and her eyes filled with tears, which never spilled onto her perfectly made-up face. "Darling, I came to help. But I can see you want to be alone. You know where to find me if you need me."

She passed Sheila in the doorway. Would there be no end to his torment! he thought.

Sheila took one look at him and stopped. "How's Tamara? Still no memory? You know, if I put this in our show, the critics would say it was unbelievable. See, truth is stranger than fiction. I'll have those contracts for you to look over at lunch." She turned and left.

Slowly, he turned to Tracy. She stared at him, a model of candor and compassion. He clenched his jaw so hard the tension radiated to his shoulders.

"If this is all a show for my benefit, Tracy, I swear I'll strangle someone!"

TAMARA STOOD with her ear pressed to the door. She could hear what everyone was saying. She didn't want to miss a thing, since even the tiniest detail could be important. Michael's parting shot pushed her away from the wood for fear he could hear her heart pounding through it.

Riddled by doubts, she fumbled with the ties to the ugly green gown, pulling it off and her evening dress back on. Had she accomplished anything by her little charade? There hadn't been the tiniest softening in Michael, not even when she'd "spilled her guts," as he'd put it. Yes, there had been a glimmer of something in his eyes, except it hadn't reassured her; it had frightened her with its intensity.

Maybe she was wrong. Maybe this foolish plan was pure crazy desperation. On the other hand, she was wild with happiness that he would sacrifice so much for her, even if at the moment he was so angry he was acting like an idiot.

Why couldn't she just tell him she knew what Jackie had done and that she wouldn't let him sacrifice himself for her?

Because he was a man! She knew he wouldn't listen right now. Hurt, pride and a million other totally male attributes she didn't understand stood in the way.

She ran her fingers through her tangled hair as she searched under the bed for her high heels. There wasn't any time to waste. Somehow, she had to stop him from signing that contract during lunch.

By the time she'd showered and changed, the morning was half gone and all the passengers should have been settled nicely in some activity. A message from Captain Swevsen waited for her in her office, ordering her to take the day off to recover. That really made her feel guilty. Here she was, lying to everyone on the ship! But she couldn't, wouldn't, back off from seeing this through.

At her most noble, she decided that even if Michael didn't forgive her, this ruse would be worthwhile if he just didn't give up his chance to direct. On the other hand, she knew if she didn't recapture the magic they'd shared so briefly, she'd shrivel up and die.

Then her common sense kicked in. Nobody died from a broken heart—it just seemed that way. She'd take it one step at a time and keep her fingers crossed.

She waited until one o'clock. She didn't want to appear overeager. Most of the lunch crowd had deserted the dining room for sunbathing on deck. Waiters were clearing away the buffet as she made her way through the dining room to the large table where the cast usually sat. Linn sat on one side of Michael, with Sheila and Tracy. There was an empty seat next to him.

As she walked toward him, she studied his marvelous physical attributes, including his dark compelling eyes and the wonderful mouth now curled in a smile as he bent to one side to talk to Tracy. Yes, he was wonderful-looking. But that wasn't it. The memory of his exquisite touch, his tenderness, his muscled body bending over her was precious. But she knew that more than physical pleasure, Michael had opened his dreams to her. And when he'd shared his own fears and hopes, she'd recognized in him everything love can mean.

At that moment, he glanced up and saw her. His eyes widened, daring her to continue the charade.

Did he know? The thought stopped her midroom. Then she got a grip on her emotions. If he did, why would he continue to go along with it?

"Hi!" Her voice cracked and she tried to cover it by clearing her throat. "Sorry I'm late."

"We went ahead and ordered." He stood and held out the chair next to him.

Little ripples of tension started building inside her. What did he know? She looked blindly around the table for something to help her.

A thick manila envelope rested between his plate and hers. He shifted it to his lap to give her more room.

The contract! She had to make sure he didn't sign it!

Sheila pushed her shrimp salad to one side and signaled to the waiter for dessert. He brought a tray of ice cream and several toppings at the same time he brought Tamara a large spinach salad.

It couldn't have gone better if it had been camera-blocked. Tamara pushed her salad aside as the waiter reached around her with a double bowl of ice cream, chocolate and strawberry. She shifted so their hands collided, dumping a lethal combination of lettuce, avocado, dressing, chocolate and strawberry squarely into the middle of Michael's lap.

"Oh, I'm so sorry!" she gasped, snatching the envelope out of his lap and dumping the whole mess on the table in front of her, trying to extract the contracts before they became soaked through and illegible.

Apologizing profusely, the waiter rushed off to find something to clean up the mess. Tracy looked at her, thunderstruck. Slowly, a smile spread across her face. It was all Tamara could do not to jump up and confess. Could Tracy, shrewd as she was, suspect what she was up to?

At that moment, Florence, clasping a bouquet of glorious red roses, ran breathlessly up to Linn. "The fan club wanted me to give you these, as a wedding memento."

Linn swiveled around, obviously thrilled with the tribute. Tamara watched, fascinated, as Linn's hand, still holding the hot fudge pitcher, wobbled. Tracy laughingly reached to take it away from Linn before she spilled its contents, yet somehow her fingers missed the handle. As if it were happening in slow motion, Tamara just had time to push her chair out of the way as the fudge went sailing across the table, leaving a dark sticky streak across the contracts before tumbling into Michael's lap.

By this time, the rest of the table seemed dumbfounded by the comedy of errors that was taking place.

"Damn!" Michael's reaction to the lapful of hot fudge was immediate. He leapt to his feet, presenting a very interesting stain to the onlookers.

"Oh, my goodness!" Tamara stood up, promptly knocking both her own and Michael's water glasses onto the chocolate mess.

She did what came naturally. She grabbed her napkin and wiped at the sticky mess on his front, keeping her head bent so no one could see the broad smile on her face. She'd done it, and in a rather spectacular fashion, if she did say so herself.

"That's enough!" Michael's growl stilled her hand. He gripped her wrist, forcing her hand away from his body.

She took a moment to compose her expression, then looked up, all sweet innocence. Exasperation filled his eyes but that didn't match what she'd felt beneath the napkin as she wiped him down. He might be furious with her, but his body betrayed him. He still wanted her.

Slowly, he released her hand, but his gaze continued to hold her. What was going on behind those unforgiving eyes?

"There's not a chance we can salvage those papers," Sheila said.

Everyone turned to look down at the sodden chocolate mess that had once been the contract. Squinting her eyes in that unnerving way she had, Sheila examined each face around the table. Was guilt written all over her face? Tamara wondered. Is that why it seemed Sheila homed in on her?

"Well, the powers-that-be will just have to fax you another one," Tracy uttered as if the calamity were no big deal.

"It's Saturday, remember?" Again Sheila's speculative gaze settled on Tamara. "No one will be in the office until Monday morning."

"Don't worry about it, Sheila." Michael was a really good sport, she had to admit. "I'm not going anywhere. Except to my cabin to clean up!"

Sticking to him like the hot fudge smeared all over his pants, Tamara went with him, the useless napkin still clutched in one hand.

"Let me help you," she insisted, waving it like a talisman.

"No, thank you."

The words were plain but she ignored them, stepping into the elevator with him.

"Michael, don't be silly." A bubble of laughter escaped her lips and she gasped deep in her throat, trying to hold back more. "Here, let me," she whispered into his ear, feeling giddy and crazy with the absurdity of the whole thing.

This time he didn't push her hand away. Very deliberately he let her feel the swelling beneath the cloth and her stroking fingers.

The elevator doors slid open. With equal deliberation he stepped out, then held up one palm to stop her from following.

"You're not yourself yet, Tamara. Go rest, get your memory back."

"On one condition." She had some other tricks up her sleeve. "Dinner in my cabin at seven. And I won't take no for an answer."

He undressed her with his eyes, making it seem the politest of gestures. Suddenly, she couldn't look at him another minute without kissing him until he came to his senses. She pushed the button to close the doors. But at the last minute, she couldn't resist.

"I promise, no hot fudge!"

"Déjà vu." Michael laughed under his breath as he let the hot water of the shower pour over his head. With a soapy cloth he washed away the stickiness that had permeated his cotton slacks, thinking all the while of Tamara and the result of her ministrations.

Cursing, he swung the faucet over to C and let the cold water cascade off his shoulders and dampen his enthusiasm. Shivering, he left the shower stall, wrapped a dry towel around his hips and stepped into the bedroom.

There was Jackie sprawled on the bed, two champagne glasses and a bottle of Dom Perignon propped against her breasts. The woman had a one-track mind and a not very inventive one! They'd been through this before.

"Now how did you get in?"

"Darling, don't glower so. You look positively demonic. Especially with your hair plastered down like that."

She undulated off the bed and wrapped her arms around his chest. "Of course, with your bone structure, you'd look magnificent bald."

Detaching her from his body caused his towel to slip. In self-defense he tightened it around his waist. "Exactly what do you want?"

"It's a celebration, darling!" The cork had already been popped, so all she had to do was fill the glasses. She licked at the champagne dripping over the edge of her flute and laughed. "Here, let's drink to another three years of Stephen Diamond, with Alexandria," she added.

Her trademark "vixen" look from under her lashes left him unmoved. Nor did he take the proffered glass.

"I'm afraid your celebration is a bit premature. I didn't sign the contract yet."

"What!" Vixen turned to shrew in a split second. He was surprised her shriek hadn't shattered the crystal.

"Calm down, Jackie. It's just a little delay because there was an accident at lunch. The copy of the contract got ruined, so Sheila has to have another faxed."

Harsh pink spots appeared on her rigid cheeks. "Who spilled what?"

"Tamara, mostly." Remembering, he couldn't help but smile. "You should have seen Sheila's face. God, what a mess. You missed a real show."

"Oh, my poor darling." She laid both palms against his cool chest, her fingers absently stroking him. "I'm afraid Tamara is still plotting against you! How desperate she must be! Faking this amnesia to use you to get into the business.''

He put her hands away from her. For some reason, her touch made him recoil.

Her lovely sapphire eyes swam with tears. ''Believe me, I've lost my memory at least six times on the show, so I can see right through her game. Can't you, darling?'' Concern and sadness filled Jackie's upturned face.

Still, he didn't believe her any more than he did Tamara. ''Don't worry, Jackie. I'm getting to the bottom of this tonight. Sooner if you'll let me get dressed.''

''Are you sure you want to get dressed . . . right now?'' Her invitation couldn't have been plainer. Luscious and ripe, she was his for the taking; but all he could think about was getting rid of her as quickly as possible.

With a firm grip on her shoulders, he propelled her to the door and opened it. ''I'll let you know what happens,'' he promised.

One gentle push was enough to allow him to shut and lock the door behind her. Then he downed both glasses of champagne before sitting on the bed to think this through.

There could be three explanations of recent events: one, Tamara loved him, regretted her lies and this was her convoluted way of trying to patch things up; two, she was, and had always been using him for another chance at the show-biz brass ring; or, three, she really had experienced a memory loss.

So what should he do? He was honest enough to admit that despite being furious and hurt, he still wanted her. As he pulled on jeans and a black *Another Hospital* T-shirt, he made up his mind.

Want didn't even come close to describing what he felt when he was with her. If he couldn't have it all *and* the truth, then he wanted nothing. There was only one way to find out. He was pretty sure that if he pressed her, she would break down and tell him everything.

But, what if she told him something so disappointing he couldn't deal with it?

TAMARA TOOK another turn around her tiny cabin, lifted the silver covers from the food again and straightened the napkins on the dining cart for the tenth time. Unlike Michael's cabin, the only place to sit while they ate dinner here would be on her bed.

Even though she expected it, the knock on her door still made her jump. Her hands were clammy and her breath grew short. The moment had come!

Although the first part of the plan had met with some success and the next would kick into action tomorrow on S&B's private island, she didn't want to contemplate why she had arranged a night like this.

Why else?

Don't think, just act! she commanded herself while opening the door.

Michael looked unpredictable, his mouth set in a hard straight line. He glanced around the room. Then he looked straight into her eyes as he closed and locked the door behind him.

She felt a hot catch at the back of her throat and her eyes burned.

"Tamara, you really should be resting."

She couldn't think of any answer that made sense. In desperation she said, "It's the meal we never had in your room that night. Remember?"

He looked over her shoulder, as if considering something. "I only remember this." He pulled her to him and kissed her in that shocking way that brought heat rushing up over her body, threatening to consume her. The kisses went on, deeper, stronger, until she became light-headed.

Then her breath stopped as his hands came to life, outlining the sides of her breasts, her waist, her hips. He made a little startled noise when he realized she wore nothing beneath her sleek knit gown of black. In one fluid motion he lifted her off her feet and onto the bed.

Yes, this was what she wanted, why she had asked him to come here. She loved the crush of him against her as he came down on top of her; loved the clean male scent that was him alone. She closed her eyes to savor the moment.

He stopped, the onslaught of kisses stilling.

She lifted her lids, heavy with desire, to study him and was stunned by the revelation in his eyes. They were large and dreamy, a spectacle of light and dark unlike anything she'd ever seen.

She knew she'd gone a little crazy. But she had never betrayed him, until now. Pain flashed through her. She hated this lie she was living, even if she did it for him. After a long soul-searching moment, she pressed a kiss on his cheek and then pushed a little at his chest.

He sat up immediately. "Something wrong, Tamara?"

"I'm . . . I'm suddenly very tired. I guess you were right. I'm sorry."

"I understand." Slowly he rose to his feet, although his eyes never left her face.

She rubbed her temple where a real headache was beginning to take shape. "Maybe everything will be back to normal tomorrow."

"Yeah, maybe tomorrow," he said so softly she barely caught the words.

Then he turned his back and left her room. Left her drowning in the awful feeling that nothing would ever be right again.

Day Eleven—S&B's Private Island

Tamara felt ready to drop from sheer exhaustion after another restless night filled with dreams and nightmares alternating between hope and despair. She was running on pure adrenaline but she had a plan to set in motion.

First, she sought out Sheila, who as usual was eating. The producer glanced up and gave Tamara an appraising look.

"You seem to be running around a great deal for someone who is supposed to be taking it easy."

"I'm feeling better and better, and since there's so much to be done with the luau, I said I'd help out." Tamara smiled ruefully, putting the proper amount of chagrin on her face. "I'd like to talk to you tonight in my office about something really important."

"Oh?" Sheila lifted her eyebrows, her eyes speculative.

"It's about that contract I ruined for you yesterday. Could you come at seven, before the luau?"

"All right. I admit I'm curious about that fiasco yesterday." Sheila nodded before going back to her breakfast. "I'll see you promptly at seven."

Tamara's next stop was the gym. The doctor had forbidden her to lead any more exercise classes but she knew Jackie would be there working out, just as the actress did every morning. She strolled through the aerobics enthusiasts to where Jackie labored on the StairMaster.

Tamara hoped her smile looked every bit as smug as Jackie's did. "I just thought I should tell you not to be so pleased with yourself. Michael isn't going to resign." She leaned closer, deliberately giving herself away. "My little *act* has taken care of that."

Jackie's face turned purple. "Why you little bit—"

Tamara cut her off with a hearty laugh that drew everyone's attention. "Tsk, tsk, Jackie, your public watches," she muttered before turning her back on the thoroughly furious prima donna. She could feel the daggers piercing her back and was certain she'd achieved the desired result.

The players were set. If only they reacted according to type.

MICHAEL STOOD at the railing watching the first launch pull away from the *Diamond Queen* and head for a deserted strip of white beach fringed by lush emerald foliage. Tamara was sitting in the bow of that boat, her blond hair highlighted by the morning sun. And while she was off, doing her job, he had some tough decisions to make.

Last night his subtle pressure had revealed nothing more than his overwhelming need. She hadn't given away one tiny secret. But her physical response had told him something. They'd come so close to making love again; surely he could attach some positive meaning to that.

Yet nothing could be the same until the truth was revealed. Tomorrow, unless something changed drastically, he'd go back to Hollywood and Tamara would go her own way.

He pushed himself away from the railing, desperate to follow her, but stubborn enough to know she must come to him. If only there was something to do, something that would keep him from catching the next launch and torturing himself with her nearness.

He decided to stroll through the lounge on the off chance one of the fans or his cast mates would be there. Anything to divert his attention.

Most of the overstuffed chairs were empty, the majority of passengers having opted to go to the island for Tamara's announced treasure hunt or just to loaf on the beach. But as he was turning to go, he caught a glimpse of a familiar face through the drooping frond of a potted palm tree. Sheila, her feet propped up, was sipping cappuccino and reading *Variety*.

She looked up from her paper, saw him and waved him over. He really had no option but to join her.

"Hi, Sheila. What's up?"

"Sit down. Don't you think it's time we talked about your contract?"

"What about it?" This wasn't going to help at all. He wanted to forget all about the decision he'd made and now Sheila was going to ask for explanations. He remained standing, propping himself against the wall and crossing his arms over his chest.

"Why do I get the feeling you weren't that upset when your contract got trashed yesterday at lunch?"

Her eyes narrowed to mere slits, pinning him right to the wall. "And why do I get the feeling you're having second thoughts about signing it?"

Straightening, he towered over her. "Because we both know it's not everything I want."

She rattled her paper at him and cut right to the bottom line. "We *know* you can be the star who will keep us number one in the ratings. But we don't know you can direct."

"When *Another Hospital* hired me, they didn't know I could act. They took a chance then!" he snapped.

"So, what are you planning to do? Sign? Or not?" she asked levelly.

"I told you I'd sign, Sheila, and I always keep my word."

She nodded, but seemed unconvinced. "I know. Even if it hurts."

That made him smile. "I always said you're one smart lady."

"Smarter than you think." She picked up her paper, deliberately opening it as wide as possible in dismissal.

Wandering aimlessly around the deck, he was aware of a sense of loss. He hadn't felt this unsure of his future in a very long time, and it scared him. If someone had asked him before this cruise if he was happy with his life, he would have answered an unequivocal yes. Now he wasn't so sure. Scratch that. Now he'd say no.

JACKIE WATCHED Michael from the bow of the ship. She'd been there for a while, but he hadn't noticed her.

He looked positively grim, his long mouth set in that hard line that made him impossible to approach. What had Tamara done now?

She decided to find Sheila and see what she could learn, much as she hated to come right out and appear to interfere. She could never quite read Sheila, whose whole attitude was based on the bottom line. If a person couldn't be manipulated, Jackie was always at a loss.

Prudently, she waited until Michael disappeared down the outside staircase before making her move.

"Sheila, darling, why are you hiding behind a plant?"

Sheila put down her mug of cappuccino and looked up, a cream mustache on her upper lip. What she wouldn't give for that metabolism!

Dabbing at her mouth with a napkin, Sheila shrugged. "I'm not hiding. I'm on vacation. That means I'm not on duty every moment."

"But you have been a busy girl, haven't you?" Draping herself in a chair, Jackie beamed her approval. "What a plume in your cap to have Michael signed, sealed and delivered for another three years."

"As my grandmother used to say back in West Virginia, 'Don't count your chickens before they're hatched.'"

Scalding anger flushed through her chest, choking her. She had to take a deep breath and count to ten to contain it. "Oh? Has something happened I should know about?"

Sheila shrugged again, but this time her eyes hardened. "I just wish he'd signed yesterday. Now I'll have to wait to see what happens."

She'd done it! That little nobody had changed his mind. Jackie wanted to throw something. Instead, she felt she had to make a graceful exit. She didn't want Sheila connecting her with this fiasco in any way.

"Oh, darling, don't fret so. It makes wrinkles." Laughing, she stood. "Trust me. I'm sure Michael will sign and everything will turn out exactly the way you want."

She bolted outside, wasting no time in finding Harry, who was in the health club sweating through a twenty-minute bike ride. She dragged him off the apparatus by the front of his red-and-black knit shirt and pulled him out into the corridor, as he protested.

"If you don't want to lose Michael, *and me,* you'd better do something fast!"

"Wh-what?" His passivity made her eyes narrow in disgust.

"Michael's getting cold feet again. I don't know what that little witch has done, but Sheila's plenty worried, I can tell you."

"What can I do?" he whined, spreading his hands in a gesture of defeat.

"*We* can, and will, do a great deal about it! Come with me and do what I say!"

The last thing she'd wanted to do this afternoon was run around a hot, humid island on an insipid treasure hunt, but Tamara was over there, and she'd find her if it was the last thing she did! Without even bothering to change or allowing Harry to clean up, she dragged him to the launch site. She finagled one of the boats ferrying passengers back and forth into taking her and Harry right away, so they wouldn't have to wait. There was no time to lose!

Once she reached the beach, there were only a few passengers reclining in the sun, and no Tamara anywhere. Finally, she caught sight of Linn, who naively directed her to her prey.

"Tamara? Oh, she's down the beach at that little thatched hut setting up the bar for tonight's luau. She's feeling a lot better today." She smiled that disgusting toothpaste-commercial smile that netted her thousands of residuals.

In no mood to play the role, Jackie spared her only a brief nod.

"Thanks, Linn. Glad to hear Tamara is feeling better," Harry muttered from behind her.

At least he was doing something besides following after her like a downtrodden dog. There wasn't a doubt in her mind that Harry had lost his usefulness to her. What a weakling!

The sight of Tamara sitting cross-legged on the palm-strewn floor of the hut looking fresh and disgustingly young while she directed the waiters in their various tasks stopped Jackie in the doorway. As always, she felt forced to play to the audience even when it was killing her.

"There you are, Tamara," she gasped, taking short little breaths as if she'd been running. "Have Harry and I missed the start of the treasure hunt?"

"Just by a few minutes." Tamara sprang to her feet, brushing sand from her sleek thighs. "I have the maps right here."

Frowning, Jackie looked down at the paper. "Darling, forgive me. I can't seem to figure this out. Can you, Harry?"

On cue, he shook his head. He looked gray, positively miserable out in the hot sun, and it served him right.

"Would you mind showing us the starting point for this delightful adventure you dreamed up?" She had to get Tamara away from an audience.

"Sure, follow me."

Tamara led them away from everybody, down the beach toward a broken-down hut that stood right at the tree line. It was a makeshift, open-sided derelict building, which groaned with every passing breeze. Inside, a spot on the sand was marked with pieces of wood arranged in an X.

"You start here and—"

"You can cut the act, Tamara!" Jackie balled the ridiculous map in her fist and tossed it in Tamara's face. "I'm not going to let some sniveling little wannabe spoil my plans! I don't know what you said or did to make Michael change his mind." Twisting her lip into a snarl, she glanced down Tamara's skinny little body. "On second thought, I know *exactly* what you did. What's your lover going to think when he finds out this little amnesia bit has been another of your lies? We know how our Michael feels about liars."

Panic widened Tamara's eyes. She darted a quick look at Harry, as if he might help her. Fool!

"I . . . I don't know what you mean."

"Sure you do. I'm going to expose you for the manipulating little witch you are."

"But it's only your word against mine." Her voice finally broke in a sob.

Jackie knew she had her on the run! All the bravado she'd displayed had vanished in the wink of an eye. Jackie moved in for the kill. Sticking her face right in Tamara's, she hissed, "You convince him to re-sign with the show or I'll blow the whistle on you."

"Oh, I see you found each other."

Oblivious to everything but her rage, Jackie had heard nothing until Linn's voice spun her around. There was another group of passengers with her who obviously wanted to start the treasure hunt. She wouldn't be able to finish her tirade with an audience, but she felt she'd made her point. Tamara was completely dismayed.

"Yes." Tamara looked from Linn to her and back as if she'd been caught in a trap. "Um, I'm afraid I can't talk right now. Why don't we discuss the... disembarkation schedule in my office tonight before we come ashore for the luau. Say, a few minutes before seven?"

Satisfied that she had Tamara exactly where she wanted her, Jackie nodded graciously and even managed a smile for the onlookers.

TAMARA TOOK a deep breath and turned back to assist the newest group of treasure hunters. That had been one of the hardest moments of the whole trip, but it had to be done. How could she keep her thoughts on her job? It was her last full day with the cruise line. But all she could think about, all her emotions were centered on just one person.

Would Michael ever be able to forgive her for what she was doing, even if it was for his own good?

She knew her best hope was that he'd be furious with everyone for a while, but when the smoke cleared she'd still be standing. Hopefully, next to him.

Doubt echoed in her head all afternoon. Even when she presented the treasure chest of prizes from the ship's boutique to Irma and Joe for finding the buried treasure—a life ring from the ship—her mind kept wandering off to seven o'clock.

The sun floated like a giant red beach ball on the horizon when she finished her job and caught the last launch back. Joe was still recording the scene with his video camera, standing in the bow of the boat. Immediately, she started toward him to warn him to sit, but then she noticed Irma had a firm grip on the back of his belt.

She hunkered down, out of his line of sight, glad there was one less thing to deal with. She was tired. This pretence stuff was harder than she'd thought it would be, particularly when people were so kind to her.

At least she'd been busy the entire day. She hadn't had time to second-guess her little plan. Just thinking of the ordeal to come made her knees feel a little weak. Her mind raced. What character flaw had made her believe all these crazy stunts would rectify her mistake? Would Michael understand that for the first time in her life she was fighting for what she wanted? He alone had given her the self-confidence to try.

But, as the meeting with Jackie loomed closer, her composure began to ebb. For some extra ammunition, she decided to forgo her official white uniform for a purple-and-red sarong. When she saw herself in the mirror, she knew she looked flamboyant, even theatrical. It pumped up her flagging courage. For good measure, she unpinned her hair and shook it out over her shoulders, then decided if she was going to go all out, why not do it up right? She stuck a red hibiscus blossom behind her ear.

She concluded she resembled someone in a B jungle movie more than an activities director trying to get into the spirit of the evening. Even so, the flashiness seemed appropriate, considering she would be dealing with Jackie.

Nerves tight, a huge weight swelling in her stomach, Tamara crept to her office, hoping no one would see her on the way. After this, she'd change back into uniform. As she opened her office door, she stopped as if a pit of vipers awaited her.

"Oh, darling, how quaint. We could be twins," Jackie cooed.

Her curving apricot lips exactly matched the color of a sarong which clung as if by magic to the swell of her breasts. She wore her hair loose with a white hibiscus over her left ear instead of the right which in native lore signified she was taken.

The clock on her wall showed a quarter to seven. Of course, this one time, Jackie would have to be early! Now she didn't have the chance to fortify herself before the real fight began. Sending a barrage of silent thoughts to Sheila to make an early appearance, Tamara forced a smile onto her face.

"I'm glad you're here. I think it's time we both laid our cards on the table." She pulled the door closed behind her, making sure to leave it open just the tiniest bit.

Only then did she notice Harry sulking in the corner; he wouldn't meet her eyes. Honestly, if these were the kinds of friends Michael had in L.A., it was no wonder he'd become such a cynic!

"Before we get started, why is Harry here? This is just between you and me." Deliberately keeping her voice soft, Tamara moved, positioning herself so she faced the door and Jackie was forced to turn toward her. She had to stall, so she threw out a red herring. "Can you trust him? Won't he tell Michael?"

"Harry's my agent, too," Jackie insisted. "And he knows what's good for me is good for him, right, Harry?"

The man nodded, looking downright miserable.

Mentally she took a deep breath. This was it. "I knew you were smart, Jackie. But how did you figure everything out so quickly?"

"Darling, you don't know who you're dealing with." Obviously preening under Tamara's admiration, Jackie tossed her head and laughed just a bit too loudly.

BORED WITH HIS ROOM, sick of his own company and his obsession with Tamara Hayes, Michael decided he'd take the first launch to the island for the farewell luau and get it over with. He had to see her sometime and he owed it to the fans to attend this last event. Thank God the cruise was ending tomorrow, before he went totally crazy.

"Hello, Mike. Are you heading to Tamara's office, too?" Sheila's question stopped him in his tracks.

"Why would I be going there?" he asked carefully.

She shrugged. "She asked me to come to discuss your contract. Naturally, I thought you'd be there."

Shrewd Sheila was fishing and he knew it but he bit, anyway. He shook his head, cursing silently. "Now what!"

"I don't know. Come with me and find out."

A thin beam of light streamed out into the corridor from Tamara's doorway. Did she realize it was open? He heard voices, recognizing Jackie's bark of laughter. Curious. What would she be doing with Tamara?

He strode confidently forward, sure he would take command of the situation at last.

"Darling, you don't know who you're dealing with. I tried to warn you away that first day. Michael is mine." Jackie's confident purr stopped him just in time.

"You had your own plans for Michael this trip, didn't you? I just was never able to figure out what they were."

Some quality in Tamara's voice made him stop, a chill creeping up his spine. Ignoring Sheila's presence, he eavesdropped without a qualm. If he had to learn the truth this way, he damn well would!

"Of course you couldn't. Harry and I are too subtle for that. You have no idea of our machinations to get him on this ship in the first place!"

Harry, too? Michael's chill turned to heat as his blood began to boil.

"But why go to such dangerous lengths to get what you want?" Tamara persisted.

He sucked in his breath, waiting. Beside him Sheila shifted closer to the open door.

"I'd do *anything* to convince him to re-sign his contract with the show! Do you have any idea how much revenue Harry would lose? And me! At this stage of my career, I'm not about to allow myself to be fired for lack of a story line." Jackie's voice rose convincingly. "It would have been simple to play to

Mike's ever-present soft spot for his old friends, except for your interference. He met you and started acting like an utter fool—waxing poetic about that foolish dream of his to direct. Utter rubbish!''

A sharp pain in his chest reminded him to let go of the breath he held. Anger poured through his veins like liquid heat.

"So you decided to discredit me after you heard me talking to Tracy. You told the newspaper hounds and they took it from there. And I played right into your hands by not telling him the whole truth myself. You used his affection for me. But blackmail, Jackie! Blackmailing him into re-signing by threatening to dredge up my past! That's not only despicable, it's a criminal offense."

"Really, darling, I must thank you for that very idea. It's quite perfect, you see. No one will ever know but us. Michael has too much pride, and *who* would ever believe *you!*"

Sheila gasped and Michael met her eyes. For once, she looked unsure of herself. But he'd heard more than enough!

With one sharp movement he pushed the door open. He only cared about one thing—Tamara's face, her eyes, her expression. He knew he'd find the truth there.

Jackie turned, stunned, as Harry gasped in surprise.

Tamara hadn't expected him. Her eyes widened, then went a flat opaque green.

The room was fraught with tension. He stood on the threshold, his hands clenched into fists at his sides, and didn't need to say a word. Harry stared at him before turning away, his shoulders slumped in defeat.

Pain for the loss of a friend sliced through him but couldn't distract him from the reason he was here.

At last Sheila found her voice. "I don't know what to say to you, Jackie. I can't in good conscience go ahead with these contract negotiations after what I've just heard."

Jackie gasped. "Don't look at me like that, Michael!" Tossing her flame curls over one bare shoulder, she flung her arm around Tamara. "You've always known what I'm capable of," she taunted. "Look at us! There isn't much to choose between Tamara and me, is there? We're both willing to lie and cheat to get what we want!"

The anguished expression on Tamara's face tore at his heart . . . what little was left of it. Then he saw beyond it, to a need he hoped he wasn't imagining. For one eerie moment he couldn't remember his anger or her betrayal.

He smiled then, a rueful tug of his mouth. "You once called me gullible, Tamara. You were right," he said in a voice so soft that it didn't sound like his. He turned to get as far away as possible from that room and the feelings ripping him apart.

WITHOUT GIVING Jackie or Sheila another thought, Tamara started after him. He seemed to disappear, he wasn't in his room or the lounge and by the time she thought of the luau, she couldn't catch him. The launch must have been waiting because it was already halfway to land before she reached the sea door.

Her worst nightmare was in full progress and she couldn't do one thing to stop it. Michael hadn't understood. She wasn't doing any of this for herself—she was doing it for him. She wanted him to recapture his dream. She wanted him to be happy. She'd do anything to make him whole again.

She paced impatiently, waiting for a launch to return. The Caribbean night was dark, a full moon and the stars were hidden by a thick layer of clouds. She felt lost in that dark, pain and fear vibrating through every inch of her.

Asking the passengers' indulgence, she stepped down into the second launch the instant it returned. She had no choices left. Forgetting pride and pain, she had to give in to the insistence of her heart. Somehow, she would find Michael and she would make him understand.

Once on the island, Tamara began to tremble with the sheer enormity of what she had to do. She could smell the fire, see the flames of the torches set out in a rectangular pattern against the dark sky. The passengers and crew members milled around within their perimeters, eating, drinking, dancing to the calypso band positioned near the buffet.

But there was no Michael.

For once, the sight of Joe, video camera to his eye, backing up dangerously close to one of the bonfires, didn't frighten her. She rushed toward him, a sob of relief catching in her throat.

"Joe, have you seen Michael Shannon?"

"I don't rightly remember, Tamara. I've been filmin' and—"

"Show me!" she demanded, grabbing the camera from him.

He pushed rewind and showed her how to fast forward. Her insides knotting in fear, she watched as launch after launch deposited people on the beach, saw the limbo contest, the roasted pig being paraded to the buffet table, the—

There he was! She froze the frame. The sea was behind him and he walked down the beach toward the ramshackle hut at the edge of the jungle.

"Thanks, Joe." She thrust the camera at him and stood on tiptoe to kiss his rough cheek.

She ran into the night, past the last of the torches, past the diminishing sounds of the music. The wind picked up, tangling her hair over her face as she ran. Her flower fell to the sand and she stepped on it, crushing it.

The sand softened, sucking at her feet, slowing her down, but she ran on, her heart pounding. This was a race she had to win.

At last she found him. He was standing with his back to her looking out over the dunes to the sea and sky, searching the endless night.

"Michael!" she called, her voice strong and determined.

He turned and she ran to him across the windswept beach. If this *were* a jungle movie, he would have caught her in his arms and rained kisses all over her body.

He didn't. Instead, he rammed his fists into the pockets of his white trousers and glared at her.

"What do you want now? To tell me you've been playing me like a fiddle since the first day we met? My

God, I'm really a fool! I even half bought into your amnesia bit!''

Suddenly, the moon broke through the cloud cover. A path of diamonds sparkled on the water behind him. She could see the sneer twisting his beautiful mouth.

When the moon disappeared again so did her patience. "How dare you! I've been running around like a crazed person, spouting bad dialogue, trying to save you from making the biggest career mistake of your life and all you can say is, 'What do you want now?' Why do I bother?''

At least she'd captured his attention. His eyes gleamed in the darkness. "Why *do* you bother?''

She trembled again, but not from fear. She dug her feet into the sand. "I love you. I love you in ways I didn't even know I could love. I bother because I'm sorry I didn't tell you the truth when I should have.'' When he didn't answer, she swallowed her pride and stepped closer. "I think giving up your dream to protect me means you love me, too. I forgive you for being too stubborn to admit it.''

She paused, but he gave her no indication what he was thinking or feeling. She balled her fists, resisting the urge to beat some sense into his hard head. "I'm sorry. And I think you should forgive me, too! We've both made mistakes. Let's not make any more. Please.''

A soft, gentle rain began to fall. Michael ignored it, staring into her eyes, accepting the truth. In the distance, lightning crackled, followed by a threatening roll of thunder. Her hands fell to her sides and tears began to fill her eyes.

It was time to stop thinking, to stop analyzing. It was time to act. To let his feelings dictate his actions. Action always spoke louder than words.

He caught her up in his arms. She was soaked with rain, but then so was he. In a few strides, he had her safely inside the tumbledown hut where the roof offered some protection from the storm.

Rain beat against the waxy palm fronds and dripped down to pool on the hard sand outside. The splash of water seemed to match the cadence of his pulse.

He kissed her, tasting tears, tasting rain, tasting Tamara. He knew he'd come home. Pleasure curled down into his throat as it had the first time they'd kissed. It would be like this always.

Laughing with sheer joy, he cupped her wet face in his hands and searched her eyes in the darkness. "You were crazy to pull such a stunt! The whole ship has been worried sick about you."

"Hush," she silenced him with small delicious kisses over his mouth and neck. "I'm sorry I worried my friends. All that matters is that it worked, didn't it?"

Without words he pulled her down onto the sand, turning so he took the graininess against his own body. Then, with no explanation, he pulled on the tie of her sarong and slowly unwound it.

He slid his mouth down her cool, sweet body, shaking with the force of his need for her. He didn't care where they were or who might come. He was lost in her and knew she was lost in the same madness.

They shed their clothes, both possessed with the same need to kiss and caress. He muttered love words, tender and sweet, and she returned them, sweeter yet.

Words that flamed the fires of their passion brighter, hotter until they were both shaking with desire. They came together, fitting perfectly, felt together the swelling ebb and flow of the heat building between them. Exploding in one exquisite instant of all-consuming pleasure, they filled each other with the power of their love.

Afterward, they dressed each other with shaky hands. Then he lifted her in his arms and she wrapped her arms around his neck as he carried her back down the beach.

TAMARA DIDN'T CARE that she was soaked with rain and tiny grains of sand rubbed against her flesh under her sarong. Michael held her in his arms.

She didn't care that passengers, huddled under golf umbrellas waiting for the launches, turned to stare when they entered the world of light and music again. She didn't care that John's eyes practically popped from his head when Michael marched right up to the oncoming launch, still carrying her in his arms.

Naturally, Joe was recording the moment for posterity and for the folks back in Omaha. She made a mental note to ask him for a copy of his tape. It would be a great pleasure to show it to her children.

Beside him, Sheila squinted at them. "I don't suppose I could speak to the two of you for a moment?"

"Not on your life." Michael barked out a short laugh. "And Sheila, I think directing six episodes the first six months of my new contract and then increasing six over each quarter should satisfy me. I'll see you tomorrow."

Tamara buried her face in his throat, feeling his pulse beneath her lips. She wanted to make love all over again, to lose herself in the feelings that made surrender so sweet.

He didn't break the long silence until he set her down in the tiny bathroom of his cabin.

"You're right. We need a shower." She laughed softly.

"Together," he said, laughing equally softly.

In the tiny stall, with the hot water beating down on them, she pressed against him, needing the feel of his lean, hard muscular body, loving every inch of him.

She looked up at him, silent and questioning. She knew now that his sizzling smile was not practiced, but just for her, which made it even more potent.

He slid his fingers into her hair and tilted her face up to meet his lips. "Every time I kiss you, it's like the first time," he whispered wonderingly. "Will it always be like this?"

She put her arms around his neck and buried her face in his shoulder. "Yes," she promised, needing nothing more.

Disembarkation

At some point during the night, they finally ended up in the bed. In the morning, she lay curled into Michael's warmth. Her body throbbed all over with odd little aches but she didn't mind at all. They'd made love on the beach, in the shower, on the floor and finally in this very bed.

She tucked her fists under her chin and snuggled deeper into contentment. She vowed it would always be like this between them. She would always feel the need to touch him, to kiss his magical mouth, to trace the contours of his strong muscles.

And he would always know how to judge her response so perfectly that he could keep them both hovering on the edge of explosion until at last, they hurdled over that edge deliberately and together.

She'd never known such a giving, caring lover. She'd never imagined that happiness could be a budding flower in her heart. She would make certain they never lost this magic.

The phone rang right beside her ear. Startled, she twisted around, grabbing for it before it could ring again and disturb him. The receiver tumbled off the hook, falling to the carpet with a loud thud. Hanging half out of the bed, she scooped it up to her ear.

"Hello," she whispered, trying not to wake him. Suddenly, she realized what she'd done, remembered where she was. Whoever was on the other end of the line would know exactly why she was answering his phone at this hour of the morning.

"I thought I'd find you there, Tamara," Sheila stated matter-of-factly. "I'm in your office. John, the purser, is looking for you. You're on duty in twenty minutes. I understand it's your last assignment for the cruise line but I need to speak with both of you as soon as possible. Is Mike available?"

She felt a delicate kiss low on her spine, then another, and yet another, moving progressively higher. A ripple of pleasure made her sigh.

"I'm sorry. He's still asleep." She told the bald-faced lie as he reached and nibbled at her earlobe. "When he wakes up, I'll tell him you called."

She dropped the receiver into its cradle and turned to his embrace. His hand stroked her throat and breasts as she leaned over him, lying against the white pillows, as if they had all the time in the world.

"I know. The world intrudes on paradise. You have to go to work, and so do I." He stopped the slow erotic exploration of his fingers and sitting forward, cupped her face with loving palms. His dark compelling eyes were no longer unreadable.

"Every time I touch you, it's as if I'm learning you for the first time." He flashed the smile that a million women swooned over daily. But for her it was, and would always be, uniquely personal. "If that sounds like bad dialogue, I won't apologize. We both know life isn't perfect, but I think this is about as close as we're going to get. So how about it? You. Me. Loving. Fighting. Loving some more. Maybe having some kids. A dog. A cat. Goldfish. What the hell, think we should take the chance, Tamara?''

Seriously wondering if anyone had ever disintegrated from happiness, Tamara giggled, trying to release some of her joy. ''I think—''

She was interrupted by a brisk knock at the door.

''Mr. Shannon, this is your stewardess. You forgot to place your baggage in the hallway last night and disembarkation is already under way. I must have it as soon as possible.''

Convulsing with laughter, they both tumbled out of bed. Disembarkation waited for no man or woman— no matter that they'd just made a commitment of sorts.

She made herself as presentable as possible while Michael appeased the flustered stewardess through the closed door. Getting hundreds of passengers off the ship, scrubbing it sparkling clean from top to bottom and fore to aft, then boarding new passengers in one day always had the staff on edge. And she was one of them, at least for the next few hours. Eluding his playful grab, she slipped out his door, saying, ''I think you'll have to wait until after the commercial for your answer.'' Laughing, she blew him kisses all the way down the hall.

Exactly twenty minutes later, she slipped into place next to John. He looked pointedly at his wristwatch, then slid her a cool reprimand out of narrowed eyes. This morning his disapproval barely registered. Nothing could penetrate her euphoria.

She smiled as the passengers streamed past all the crew members lined up to bid them farewell, not because she had to, but because she couldn't have stopped if she'd wanted to.

Eileen and Shirley left arm in arm with their pharmacists. The world was certainly a happy place this morning.

She knew the disembarkation schedule by heart. Fans first, then when the commotion died down and the press were in place, the *Another Hospital* contingent would leave.

And she would be with them.

Surely Michael couldn't doubt her answer to his proposal. He had looked so serious and so beautiful, his face still flushed with sleep, but his eyes alert to the possibilities his hands were discovering.

She'd been too stunned to answer for a second and then she'd been interrupted. It had been almost impossible to leave him, and the second she got off duty, she'd find him and tell him, yes, yes, *yes!*

Irma and Joe stopped to shake her hand. "That nice Miss Peterson is takin' my film and makin' copies for everyone in the fan club back home." Joe's chest puffed out in pride. "I'd like to send you one."

"You can reach me through the S&B cruise line. I'll be moving very soon."

"Maybe to the West Coast?" Irma, grinning from one dangling gold earring to the other, quivered with excitement.

Had they really been that obvious?

"Maybe." Tamara laughed, embarrassed and elated at the same time.

"If I have anything to say about it, the answer most definitely will be yes." Michael had sneaked up behind her, and in a second, his arms closed around her for everyone to see. Proudly, she looked up at him, openly admitting their relationship to the world. Her heart pounded and excitement tingled to her fingertips.

Joe and Irma congratulated them before starting down the gangplank. As usual, Joe began filming, but Irma kept a firm hand on his arm until they reached solid ground.

The barricades were in place and most of the passengers had moved away when, hand in hand, Linn and Wayne descended the gangplank in style. They were immediately surrounded by the media, full of questions about the unanticipated wedding.

Next came Tracy with Florence, who both looked very pleased with themselves.

"I finally got Florence to agree to be my personal assistant," Tracy crowed. "At last I'll have someone who'll know what I'm talking about when I reminisce and who doesn't have a radio blaring hard rock in their ears constantly."

Florence's pleased chuckle made Tamara smile. "I'm too young to be retired. I've decided I'm not too old to try new things and broaden my horizon."

"If doll-face doesn't make you happy, hon, he'll have us both to deal with!"

She felt Michael's body shake with silent laughter at Tracy's broad wink.

"We'll see you both at home," he called after them.

Out of the corner of her eye, she glimpsed Jackie, dressed to kill for departure. She was in shocking pink, calculated to draw all eyes to her, wearing an enormous straw hat. Her steward followed a few steps behind lugging all her Vuitton luggage. She moved majestically through the crowd, playing them for all the attention she could get. Harry was nowhere to be seen.

Tamara turned around to see Michael's reaction. He was deep in conversation with the captain and hadn't even noticed his costar's extravagant display.

"Excuse me. Do you think the two of you could at last give me a few seconds of your valuable time?" Sheila positioned herself directly in front of them and by the look on her face wouldn't take no for an answer.

Defiance widened Michael's eyes. He pulled Tamara tightly to his side in a protective gesture, daring Sheila to make whatever she wanted out of it.

"I told you what I want, Sheila. I won't settle for less."

"How about more?" She thrust a stapled stack of papers at him. "Look it over. It starts with ten directorial opportunities the first quarter and increases five each quarter for four years, instead of three." She shrugged. "We give you something more, you give us something more. Seems fair to me."

He put out one hand to take the contract while keeping the other securely around her.

Sheila ignored him, leaning forward to talk to her directly. "And this is for you." She held out another stack of papers.

Automatically Tamara took them. She gasped. "This is a contract to appear on your show."

She glanced at Michael, who looked as stunned as she felt, then turned slowly back to Sheila.

"I have your screen test on tape. The powers-that-be trust my judgment, but I'm taking Joe's footage to show them, anyway. I want everyone to agree with my new story idea. Stephen Diamond finally meets his match."

Here was her dream—in the palm of her hand. And Michael had his dream. Together they would forge a new dream that would last them all the days of their lives.

She stared Sheila straight in the eye. "What about the unwritten rule? I plan to be Mrs. Michael Shannon in a few days."

He pulled her around to place a wonderful, sweet, hot kiss on her mouth. She tried to push him away but he wouldn't stop kissing her.

"Tamara, you'll do it! You'll marry me?" He stopped to take a breath. "Let's go, right now, before you change your mind!"

She squealed when he swung her up in his arms. Clutching both contracts to her bosom, she laughed. "Well, Sheila, you see how it is."

"I've seen for a week. And so has everyone else. Between the two of you, and Linn and Wayne, we're changing the unwritten rule. Now we're the soap with couples that are so hot they're for real."

Tamara couldn't believe what was happening to her. She had to hold tight as he made his way down onto the pier, swaggering as if he were a pirate and she his booty. The crowd stared openmouthed at them, but he wouldn't listen to any of her protestations.

The instant the press caught sight of him, they flocked over, deserting Jackie, and began throwing questions at them from all sides, which Michael answered with incredible good humor.

Held high against Michael's chest, she could see over everyone's head to where Jackie stood, abandoned, at the pier's edge. Fury was written plainly across her face. Then she watched as Jackie took a long calculating glance down at the water, saw the instant she made up her mind.

"Michael!"

Jackie's piercing scream snapped every head toward her. She'd hardly disappeared off the edge before six men jumped in to save her. Every reporter and newsman rushed to the edge of the pier and peered down.

"Just what she wants, all the attention focused on her. Trust me, she'll be fine."

She met Michael's sparkling sunlit eyes and couldn't resist kissing him. "I only had one man jump in after me. But I got the prize—the Diamond man!"

Laughing, he kissed her mouth. "I don't know if I'm much of a prize, but you're stuck with me for good. *And* it looks like you're stuck with Stephen Diamond for the next four years. What do you think of that, Mrs. Shannon?"

Ever so gently she bit at his earlobe. "I think Sheila's right. Both you *and* Mr. Diamond have met your match."

HARLEQUIN® AMERICAN ROMANCE®

COMING NEXT MONTH

#553 THE MARRYING TYPE by Judith Arnold
Like his friends, Steve Chambliss vowed to be a bachelor forever. Then he appeared
on "The Gwen Talbot Show"—and fell hard for the hostess herself. She didn't mix
business with pleasure, and confirmed bachelors didn't mix lust with love...or did
they? *Don't miss the first book in the Studs series!*

#554 THE INVISIBLE GROOM by Barbara Bretton
More Than Men
Saying "I do" might be the hardest thing Chase Quinn ever had to do—but it was the
only way he'd be free of the curse that rendered him invisible. Only thing was, the see-
through playboy had to *mean* it!

#555 FINDING DADDY by Judy Christenberry
Kelly Abbott needed a baby—she didn't need or want the man who came
along with it. Trouble was, the only guy who met all her requirements—
James Townsend—had designs on being a full-time hubby and daddy!

#556 LOVE POTION #5 by Cathy Gillen Thacker
As far as Remy Beauregard was concerned, Jill Sutherland was nothing more than a
Yankee career woman with too much attitude—until he accidentally drank a love
potion. With every gulp, Jill looked better...until Remy found himself agreeing to a
steamy bayou trek. Unfortunately, the antidote Jill sought was now the last thing on
Remy's mind.

AVAILABLE THIS MONTH:

#549 THE WEDDING GAMBLE
Muriel Jensen

#550 SEDUCING SPENCER
Nikki Rivers

#551 CRUISIN' MR. DIAMOND
Lynn Leslie

#552 THE PAUPER AND THE PRINCESS
Karen Toller Whittenburg

1994 MISTLETOE MARRIAGES
HISTORICAL CHRISTMAS STORIES

With a twinkle of lights and a flurry of snowflakes, Harlequin Historicals presents *Mistletoe Marriages*, a collection of four of the most magical stories by your favorite historical authors. The perfect way to celebrate the season!

Brimming with romance and good cheer, these heartwarming stories will be available in November wherever Harlequin books are sold.

RENDEZVOUS by Elaine Barbieri
THE WOLF AND THE LAMB by Kathleen Eagle
CHRISTMAS IN THE VALLEY by Margaret Moore
KEEPING CHRISTMAS by Patricia Gardner Evans

Add a touch of romance to your holiday with *Mistletoe Marriages* Christmas Stories!

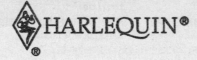

HARLEQUIN®
AMERICAN ◆ ROMANCE®

You asked for it...you've got it. More MEN!

MORE THAN MEN

We're thrilled to bring you another special edition of the popular MORE THAN MEN series.

Like those who have come before him, Chase Quinn is more than tall, dark and handsome. All of these men have extraordinary powers that make them "more than men." But whether they are able to grant you three wishes or live forever, make no mistake—their greatest, most extraordinary power is of seduction.

So make a date in October with Chase Quinn in

#554 THE INVISIBLE GROOM
by Barbara Bretton

SUPH6

This summer, come cruising with Harlequin Books!

PORTS
OF CALL

In July, August and September, excitement, danger and, of course, romance can be found in Lynn Leslie's exciting new miniseries PORTS OF CALL. Not only can you cruise the South Pacific, the Caribbean and the Nile, your journey will also take you to Harlequin Superromance®, Harlequin Intrigue® and Harlequin American Romance®.

- ♦ In July, cruise the South Pacific with SINGAPORE FLING, a Harlequin Superromance
- ♦ NIGHT OF THE NILE from Harlequin Intrigue will heat up your August
- ♦ September is the perfect month for CRUISIN' MR. DIAMOND from Harlequin American Romance

So, cruise through the summer with LYNN LESLIE and HARLEQUIN BOOKS!

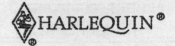

THE VENGEFUL GROOM
Sara Wood

Legend has it that those married in Eternity's chapel are destined for a lifetime of happiness. But happiness isn't what Giovanni wants from marriage—it's revenge!

Ten years ago, Tina's testimony sent Gio to prison—for a crime he didn't commit. *Now* he's back in Eternity and looking for a bride. *Now* Tina is about to learn just how ruthless and disturbingly sensual Gio's brand of vengeance can be.

THE VENGEFUL GROOM, available in October from Harlequin Presents, is the fifth book in Harlequin's new cross-line series, **WEDDINGS, INC.** Be sure to look for the sixth book, **EDGE OF ETERNITY,** by Jasmine Cresswell (Harlequin Intrigue #298), coming in November.

WED5

HARLEQUIN®

AMERICAN ◆ ROMANCE®

Four sexy hunks who vowed they'd never take "the vow" of marriage...

What happens to this Bachelor Club when, one by one, they find the right bachelorette?

Meet four of the most perfect men:

Steve: **THE MARRYING TYPE**
Judith Arnold
(October)

Tripp: **ONCE UPON A HONEYMOON**
Julie Kistler
(November)

Ukiah: **HE'S A REBEL**
Linda Randall Wisdom
(December)

Deke: **THE WORLD'S LAST BACHELOR**
Pamela Browning
(January)

This September, discover the fun of falling in love with...

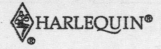

Harlequin is pleased to bring you this exciting new collection of three original short stories by bestselling authors!

ELISE TITLE
BARBARA BRETTON
LASS SMALL

LOVE AND LAUGHTER—sexy, romantic, fun stories guaranteed to tickle your funny bone and fuel your fantasies!

Available in September wherever Harlequin books are sold.

◆HARLEQUIN®

HARLEQUIN®

Don't miss these Harlequin favorites by some of our most
distinguished authors!
And now you can receive a discount by ordering two or more titles!

HT #25525	THE PERFECT HUSBAND by Kristine Rolofson	$2.99	☐
HT #25554	LOVERS' SECRETS by Glenda Sanders	$2.99	☐
HP #11577	THE STONE PRINCESS by Robyn Donald	$2.99	☐
HP #11554	SECRET ADMIRER by Susan Napier	$2.99	☐
HR #03277	THE LADY AND THE TOMCAT by Bethany Campbell	$2.99	☐
HR #03283	FOREIGN AFFAIR by Eva Rutland	$2.99	☐
HS #70529	KEEPING CHRISTMAS by Marisa Carroll	$3.39	☐
HS #70578	THE LAST BUCCANEER by Lynn Erickson	$3.50	☐
HI #22256	THRICE FAMILIAR by Caroline Burnes	$2.99	☐
HI #22238	PRESUMED GUILTY by Tess Gerritsen	$2.99	☐
HAR #16496	OH, YOU BEAUTIFUL DOLL by Judith Arnold	$3.50	☐
HAR #16510	WED AGAIN by Elda Minger	$3.50	☐
HH #28719	RACHEL by Lynda Trent	$3.99	☐
HH #28795	PIECES OF SKY by Marianne Willman	$3.99	☐

Harlequin Promotional Titles

#97122	LINGERING SHADOWS by Penny Jordan	$5.99	☐
	(limited quantities available on certain titles)		

	AMOUNT	$
DEDUCT:	**10% DISCOUNT FOR 2+ BOOKS**	$
	POSTAGE & HANDLING	$
	($1.00 for one book, 50¢ for each additional)	
	APPLICABLE TAXES*	$＿＿＿＿
	TOTAL PAYABLE	$＿＿＿＿
	(check or money order—please do not send cash)	

To order, complete this form and send it, along with a check or money order for the
total above, payable to Harlequin Books, to: **In the U.S.:** 3010 Walden Avenue,
P.O. Box 9047, Buffalo, NY 14269-9047; **In Canada:** P.O. Box 613, Fort Erie, Ontario,
L2A 5X3.

Name: ＿＿＿＿＿＿＿＿＿＿＿＿＿＿＿＿＿＿＿＿＿＿＿＿＿＿＿＿＿＿

Address: ＿＿＿＿＿＿＿＿＿＿＿＿City: ＿＿＿＿＿＿＿＿＿＿

State/Prov.: ＿＿＿＿＿＿＿ Zip/Postal Code: ＿＿＿＿＿＿＿＿

*New York residents remit applicable sales taxes.
Canadian residents remit applicable GST and provincial taxes..

HBACK-JS